Stilettos On The Run

Stilettos On The Run

C.L. BAUER

Stilettos On The Run Copyright © 2022 by C.L. Bauer.

All rights reserved. Printed in the United States of America. No part of this book may be used or reproduced in any manner whatsoever without written permission except in the case of brief quotations embodied in critical articles or reviews.

This book is a work of fiction. Names, characters, businesses, organizations, places, events and incidents either are the product of the author's imagination or are used fictitiously. Any resemblance to actual persons, living or dead, events, or locales is entirely coincidental.

For information contact:

www.clbauer.com

Cover Art By: Carolyn Schneck
Design: Miller Publishing LLC

ISBN: 979-8-218-00348-7

First Edition: April 2022

10 9 8 7 6 5 4 3 2

The Lily List Mystery Series

The Poppy Drop
The Hibiscus Heist
The Tulip Terror
The Sweet Pea Secret
The Magnolia Dilemma

The Lily List Mystery Exclusives

Stilettos Can Be Murder
Stilettos On The Run

Dedication

To joy and freedom, two attributes of this main character. I continue to appreciate my family and friends who support me in so many ways. A big thanks to KS for this great title and for T, a friend and fan.

Chapter One

"Daniel, my dear detective, do you really need to go?" Gretchen Malloy's question contained a breath of uncertainty. She wasn't used to a man leaving her in the middle of the night, yet this one already had one foot out her door. *This just doesn't make sense.*

The detective intrigued Gretchen from the moment she had looked into those gray eyes months ago. He was questioning her in a murder case and had assumed she was guilty of said murder, but obviously she'd won him over. He had been waiting outside her apartment. She'd just dropped her life-long love at the airport. It was amusing that she left one man, and another was just waiting on the sidewalk for her. *I love my life!*

Detective Daniel Williams smiled sweetly, his dimples dimpling. It would be so easy to just stay, but he absolutely needed to leave. He needed to leave now before he changed his mind. He never rushed, and he was never rash. Slow and steady kept him out of trouble, and this woman was trouble. Only a few weeks ago this event planner was the number one suspect in his high-profile murder investigation of a dead groom.

He hadn't planned on staying so late, but it was surprisingly easy to talk to her for hours. Talking with a woman had never been his strong suit, at least that's what his former wife always said. But she'd never watched him interrogate a female suspect. Williams glanced at his watch.

"Ms. Malloy, it's almost four in the morning. I've been here since, well, yesterday afternoon. You must be tired of me by now."

Gretchen coyly leaned on the other side of the door, stretching one leg forward to elongate her figure. She ran her tongue seductively over her full lips. "I'm not sure I would ever tire of you, and I thought we were calling each other by our first names. We settled that over two hours ago if you recall. You have stayed the night with me; besides, we have shared so much. Sharing just a little bit more wouldn't hurt anyone. I've found it never has so far." Gretchen winked in case he hadn't caught her innuendo.

Williams pulled his car key quickly from his pocket. His hand began to shake. He needed to get out of here before he broke. "Gretchen, I'm leaving. I haven't stayed the night with you."

Gretchen moistened her lips again with a slide of her tongue. She fluttered her overly mascaraed eyelashes. *He's a tough nut to crack! But what fun that would be to try!* "You can't think of a time when you might?"

"Is that an invitation?" He could play this game too. He was a highly esteemed detective. *Then, if I'm so confident, why are my hands still shaking?*

Gretchen's heart quickened. She lifted one of her legs to balance it on the wall as though she was the perfect flirty flamingo. "Do you want it to be, Daniel?"

Williams lowered his glance. His mouth was dry when he murmured an answer. "Tonight, I need to go."

Gretchen lowered her leg and moved away from her support. Her tone changed as though she was in a meeting with her financial advisor. "Ah, I see. A friendship is a good thing to cultivate. I understand completely. We do have a slight age difference, and we do come from different backgrounds."

Williams managed to clear his throat and stand a little taller. He felt as though a glove had been thrown down at his feet as a challenge. He wasn't one to back down. As his confidence and restraint steeled, he figured he could play this game. He closed the space between them and looked into her eyes. "It doesn't matter where we come from. What matters is now. As for an age difference, I know how old you are. I'm younger. When has age ever mattered to you?"

Gretchen pretended to be preoccupied with her fingernails. *I do need a manicure.* "Age doesn't matter between friends. Obviously, we can talk for hours and there's some sort of attraction, but male friends are good to have. I've realized over the years that female conversation can be highly overrated."

Daniel Williams was not one who backed away from any challenge, not that Gretchen was one. She was an enigma. Before he retreated from her apartment, he needed to decide what this woman could be to him. She could be infuriating, irritating, and drive him insane beyond reason. But she was also attractive, intelligent, funny and highly entertaining. He was drawn to her in so many ways and beyond reason. There was a joy surrounding her even though he had learned during the investigation that her life hadn't always been rainbows and unicorns. She had her share of strife and sorrow. He understood those emotions more than most.

Williams took a deep breath as though he were ready to dive into deep water. Quickly, before he changed his mind, he closed the space between them. His determined steps pushed her back into the living room. Sweeping her up into his arms, confusion struck in Gretchen's face. He looked into her eyes and wondered how he hadn't noticed those amazing moons of deep chocolate brown before. He wanted to take a tissue to them and remove all the makeup to see what she really looked like when she was this close to a man. Thankfully, her lips were barely tinted with her signature red lipstick.

"Detective? Daniel? What is it?"

"We can be friends, but–" He leaned down impetuously and melted his lips upon hers without another second of thought. It seemed like the thing to do.

My, my, my! Gretchen could usually think of other things while being kissed, such as what to have for dinner, what was on her calendar for the next day, or did she really need another pair of leopard print stilettos? But she had no thoughts except how much she didn't want this man to leave. *If he can provoke such feelings like this with only his lips?* She pressed her body closer into his chest. As she wrapped her arms around his neck, he changed his hold to the hollow of her back. Slowly, he pulled away begrudgingly.

"I really do need to go."

"Daniel, where did you learn to kiss like that?" Gretchen took in oxygen. He had literally left her breathless and unnerved. "At detective school?"

Williams flushed as he retreated. "Um, no. I'll tell you some other time. Goodnight, Gretchen. Thank you for dinner and a wonderful evening."

As he exited into the hallway, Gretchen stepped out. "And for that kiss?"

He winked and turned toward the elevator. "I believe you should be thanking me, Ms. Malloy."

And he's smart too! "As well I should. I'll do it the next time I see you, and I'll do it in my own special way."

He chuckled as the elevator door opened. He saluted her. "I'll be looking forward to it."

The door closed, and he was gone. Gretchen turned back into her home and shut the door firmly. "I will too, Daniel. I'll be looking forward to more kisses and praying for more than a few lip locks."

Daniel Williams chuckled all the way down to his car in the garage. He shook his head, wondering what the heck he was getting himself into.

"What is it about her?" he asked out loud. "She makes me laugh." He hadn't laughed with anyone in so long, nor had he talked for hours about everything from architecture to music. He vaguely remembered a discussion about the penguins at the zoo, but that was during the wine portion of the night. It seemed as though Gretchen did everything well, even making him the best cup of coffee he'd had since well, ever.

As he drove out onto Wornall Road, he saw the first police car race though the Plaza. By the time he saw the second and third patrol vehicles, he began to follow. They were surrounding one of the large stores in the shopping area. Williams parked his car away from the scene and walked in. He flashed his badge. Thankfully, he noticed a detective he knew.

"Beckham, what's going on?"

Randy Beckham glanced up from his phone. "Williams? What are you doing here?"

"I was visiting a friend and saw the action." *I was visiting a friend? Geez, Williams, you sound like a teenager who doesn't want to get caught visiting the loose girl of the cheerleading squad. The next thing you know you'll be explaining how she had a lightbulb that needed to be replaced at midnight.*

"Another kid has died. His body was found in the alley between the jewelry store and Laurent's department store. It's funny. I didn't even know this little jewelry place was here."

Daniel did. He knew Bouchet's very well. They only sold high-end merchandise. "Do we know the kid?"

"You might know him. I know you still work with that urban group. He was wearing one of their hoodies."

Daniel grimaced. "May I take a look?"

Beckham nodded. "Sure. It could help us. He had no identification, no phone, nothing."

Beckham shoved through the other officers and the incoming forensic crew to lead Williams to the victim's body. As the two men arrived, Daniel saw the body of a boy in his late teens. His eyes were wide open, and his head turned slightly to the side. His left leg was bent back in a distorted manner; his left arm hidden under his body. The other side of his body was more relaxed, both leg and arm straight out on the concrete.

"He looks like he was thrown out," Daniel decided. He took a couple steps closer and reached back for Beckham's flashlight. Crouching down, he pointed the light in the body's direction for a closer look. He saw the name on the hoodie–Crusaders. He had given those out to some of the senior leaders for the basketball teams. He moved the light up to illuminate the victim's face.

Daniel's stomach lurched. Acid filled his throat, and he swallowed hard to choke it back. "Jesus." He hung his head down. "Why?" He stood up slowly and turned to Beckham.

"His name is Tito King. He's one of my very best kids."

Beckham plugged the name into his notes. "You can't save all of them, Williams."

All breath escaped Daniel's body. The heavy sigh was audible to several of the men and women doing their jobs around him. Daniel handed the flashlight back to Beckham and motioned him away from the crime scene.

"What? What's up?" Beckham could see the confusion on the other detective's face.

"Look, that kid was saved. He had a job. He had a girlfriend. He wasn't on drugs, in fact…" He stopped short of relaying the remainder of Tito's story. "Beckham, just trust me on this. This was a good kid."

"I believe you, but then how did he end up here in this alley? Are we looking at a problem here in the most expensive shopping area in the city? If we are, this is a big thing."

"It's a big thing no matter where it is," Williams admitted. "Just because that shop sells diamonds to wealthy people doesn't mean Tito's life had any less value than those jewels. I get sick and tired of that kind of thinking. We have problems all over the city, but it seems money always drives the solution."

"You don't need to preach to me," Beckham responded quickly. "You think this kid was good, then explain to me how he ended up dead in what looks like a gang retaliation." He pointed back to the swarm of investigators in the alley. "You know that's how all of them will treat it. It's the obvious answer."

Surprisingly, Daniel smiled. "People always see what they want to see, don't they? Take me, I'm not who I seem, but I show you who I want you to see. I'll send you a secure email in the morning explaining who Tito was. I need to go to bed before I say too much."

Beckham was completely confused as he watched Detective Williams walk away.

As Daniel drove home, he bit the side of his mouth to contain his anger. He slammed his fist on the steering wheel. Nothing was working at curbing his temper. His co-workers weren't bad people, perhaps overwhelmed, but not bad. But they would take the obvious route, and that was perfectly understandable. He might have done the same thing except he knew Tito. He had taken the time to understand the young man. He knew Tito's devotion to his grandparents. He knew Tito's job was everything to him. Daniel knew that Tito had been working with the KCPD gang unit as an informant. Tito was taking a course in criminal law, and he'd already spoken with the FBI to make his future happen. Tito wanted a future, and now all of that was in the past forever.

"A perfectly wonderful evening turned to garbage because I had to follow those police cars."

Was anything saved from tonight? Daniel's thoughts were an attempt to temper his anger. *I have probably found the only woman in town who doesn't judge someone on their job or their looks, or even how much money they make. It's a surprise since she is so, so…*

"Gretchen." Daniel Williams smiled, feeling his anger ebbing. *What have I gotten myself into?*

Chapter Two

Gretchen hardly ever slept past seven in the morning, but to her surprise, her eyes opened to a full sun exposed in its sky. She stretched and yawned before she glanced over at her clock beside the bed.

"It's almost nine." *When have I ever been this tired without...*

"Never," she said out loud. "Detective Williams, you left me exhausted, and all we did was talk. And you kissed me." After she accepted that he was leaving her after hours of laughing and sharing a meal, he surprised her with that kiss. It was as though he was stalling as he stood in that doorway. *What would've made him stay? Had he wanted to stay? That man makes me crazy! He's making me doubt myself and all of my attributes, and I never do that.*

Gretchen showered, ate a light breakfast, and checked her schedule. It was Saturday, and she had a weekend off. This weekend was historically quiet. Even though it was still considered summer, the warm weather was waning. Colleges were opening, there were festivals all over the city, and most couples were preparing for their fall weddings. She looked ahead to next week. She had two consultations and a sit-down with a charity for an upcoming event.

Any scent of scandal about her after this summer's murder at one of her weddings had disappeared. It was good to be Gretchen Malloy. *Especially after that kiss!* The detective had certainly held his own with the best of kissers, and she had rated many over the years. Of course, her long standing love, Chance was number one on the list, but that was because he was familiar and comfortable. *There was that soccer player in Italy…*

"What am I going to do?" Gretchen walked around her apartment. Heading out onto her balcony to finish her coffee, Gretchen leaned over to see the Plaza at her feet. She sighed. "I need to do something. I just can't allow him to kiss me senseless and then do nothing."

She sat down and took a sip from her cup. *Shopping might make me feel better. I could use a pair of navy-blue heels. I don't have any, do I? But I'm just confused. I should call Lily.*

Gretchen headed inside and grabbed her phone to call Lily in Virginia. Instead of her friend, Lily's husband unexpectedly answered.

"Hello."

"Devlin, is that you?"

"Yes, Gretchen," Devlin Pierce acknowledged.

"May I speak with your lovely wife?"

"Gretchen, may she call you back? She's a little busy right now." Dev waited for a response. "Gretchen, can I do something for you?"

Could he? Could Mr. Delicious really understand my plight? "I'm not sure. You know, usually, well almost always, I can handle just about any situation, but frankly I'm completely frazzled."

In Virginia, Devlin Pierce was completely confused. "Gretchen, what's causing you such discomfort?"

Gretchen's laughter was exaggerated with her nervousness. "A man, of course. Isn't it always a man?"

"In my case, it's always been because of a woman," Dev answered coyly.

Gretchen needed answers. She didn't need a debate. "I like this man. He kissed me. He left. He didn't stay. He didn't even say he wanted to stay. What kind of a man does that?"

A smart one, if he knows what's good for him! "Perhaps he wants to establish a relationship first, or maybe he just wants to be good friends."

"I hate that *friend* word. Such a platonic relationship with such an attractive man is unacceptable to me."

"Gretchen, you and I are friends. It can work."

"Dear, dear boy, the only reason why we are only friends is because of dear Lily, or I would've jumped–"

"Gretchen, what didn't the man do?" Dev questioned quickly before he received more vivid descriptions that could haunt his nightmares.

As her mind raced in thought, Gretchen debated with her inner demons. "Well, he didn't do anything. Well, he did, but he didn't. Most men always want to do something. But he's younger. Maybe he's feeling insecure, or perhaps it's because I have more money. He's a police detective. There's also the fact that I can be a bit much."

Dev chuckled. "You think? You can be a lot too much. In fact, you're more complicated than some drug lords I've met. Wait, did you say he's younger than you?"

"Yes, by just a few years," Gretchen lied, at least she thought she was fibbing. Daniel had the body of a man in his thirties, but his peppered hair inferred he was older. At least she actually hoped he was. It was one thing to dally with a boytoy for a brief time, but she wanted the detective to be around awhile longer. "But should age matter?"

"Exactly," Dev answered quickly. "Why don't you just give him some time? Besides, are you really looking for a relationship?"

"Am I?" Gretchen murmured.

"Gretchen? Are you still there?" Dev began to worry. He never thought he would ever hear Gretchen admit her vulnerability. *Who is this guy? He must be some god or off his meds.*

"I'm here," she finally answered. "Dev, don't tell Lily about this. I have a reputation to uphold, and it's not one of babbling fool. I shouldn't have called."

Dev did hear vulnerability in her voice, or perhaps some misplaced lament. "Gretchen, are you lonely? Are you okay?"

Gretchen sniffed. She swept away a tear. "Please tell Lily I'm okay. If she knew I called, and I'm crying, she would be worried about me."

Dev said a silent prayer. "Please don't cry. I don't know how you're feeling, but it's okay to be lonely. Most people admit it long before now."

"But I'm not normal!"

Dev brought his fist up to his mouth. He had a choice. He could say yes, or he could say no. The woman wasn't normal, was she? *No, she isn't.* "Gretchen, call him. That's what the Gretchen Malloy I know would do. She would ask him out, but don't make it a romantic dinner. Just go out and have a good time."

"I have baseball tickets for tomorrow. I could ask him to go with me." Gretchen's tears were vanquished by a divine idea.

"Excellent," Dev praised. "That is perfect. Don't get down if he says no. He might be busy on such short notice. Don't get upset." *If he were bright, the man would say he had to work even if he was on the golf course all day.*

"Thank you. This must seem silly to you."

"Not at all," Dev lied. *It all sounds perfectly normal if we were all in high school again.*

"Mr. Delicious, I must go. I need to call a very special man. Thank you. Oh, and Devlin, I'm still waiting on a baby girl to spoil. Don't forget. Ta."

Dev pretended to hit his head on the living room wall in frustration. Before he could answer, not knowing really what to say, Gretchen was gone. His wife walked by him.

"Why are you doing that?" Lily asked calmly.

"I was handling your friend, Gretchen," Dev admitted.

Lily giggled. "Really? That's highly unusual. No man ever handles Gretchen." Lily began to laugh out loud.

"I take that back. A man can handle her, only if she lets him."

"It seems she wants some detective to handle her. Now that I've said that I'll have that image in my head." Dev shook his head. "I'm going to pray for that poor guy. He's going to have his hands full with the stiletto terrorist."

Chapter Three

"Daniel, I have tickets for tomorrow's baseball game. Would you like to go with me?" Gretchen's voice faltered. *I sound like a lovesick teenager. Get a grip, old girl. You are Gretchen Malloy, and you do not beg!*

The brief silence ate away at the usually overly confident coordinator. Daniel paused over his keyboard. He was just about to send a very important email to Detective Beckham. "Ms. Malloy, that's something I might be interested in."

Gretchen's heart sank. *Ms. Malloy? Something of interest, really?* "It's a one o'clock game. If you're not interested–"

"I'm at my desk. Is this something we can discuss later?"

Gretchen's heart returned to its proper location. "Oh, you're at work. I'm so sorry. Yes, later would be wonderful. Goodbye." She hung up before she could bother him any longer.

Gretchen paced around her apartment for an hour before she couldn't stand waiting any longer. She needed a new outfit for the game. Who was she kidding? She just needed a little shopping therapy. She needed to use her credit card, walk through the Plaza, and carry a shopping bag in her hand.

After grabbing a coffee at one of her favorite hangouts, she walked slowly as she surveyed the shop windows. Noticing the reflection of police tape, she turned to see the entire adjacent alley secured. She took a few steps over to the corner and looked toward the scene. Two officers seemed to be looking for something. *What is going on in my city?*

"Excuse me. What is going on?" Gretchen's voice caught the attention of the female officer. She looked up quickly and smiled.

"Gretchen? Is that really you?"

"Honey, it's always really me." Gretchen gestured down her body with one hand. "From head to toe. You look very familiar."

"Officer Alvarez, well I was Christina Paloma. You were my wedding coordinator last year. My dad is Johnnie Paloma."

Gretchen smiled. "Johnnie Paloma's little princess who carries a gun. I remember. Look at you! That uniform is very fitting on you." *Should I say she looks pretty?*

"I'll tell my dad I saw you. Who knows? You might have another wedding with all of us. Dad is finally dating a wonderful woman, and we all really like her. It took him a while to date after mom passed away, but he's happy right now."

Gretchen nodded. Now, she completely remembered. The man had lost his wife in a devastating accident on the interstate. A truck's load shifted, and Mrs. Paloma's car was flattened, killing her instantly. He had raised two daughters and two sons for almost ten years. "Good for him. Please give him my best." Gretchen pointed to the alley. "What is all of this about?"

"It was on the news this morning. A teen gang banger's body was dropped here."

"That is such a shame. There's so much more to do with your life than just drugs."

Alvarez adjusted her sunglasses. "We're back out here again this morning just in case we missed something. One of our detectives swears the kid wasn't part of a gang. He's well respected so we have to do the extra work."

"Of course you do," Gretchen said adamantly. "I was nearly framed for murder this summer. If it weren't for my own ingenuity, and for this nice Detective Williams, I'd be in the big house right now knitting a sweater for my new girlfriend Freida."

Alvarez stifled a giggle. "I did hear about that. It's funny you brought him up. Williams is who sent us back out here. Apparently, he was really torn up about the boy's death."

Gretchen's eyes narrowed. "This happened last night?"

"Sometime last night. The detective was in the area visiting a friend and noticed the activity."

The best event planner in the city clenched her entire body. The use of the word friend in reference to her was becoming a nuisance and a physical ailment to her.

"He was visiting a friend," Gretchen repeated. "How nice."

Alvarez shrugged. "It's high rent around here. It must be a very nice friend. Maybe he's finally dating someone. We don't hear personal rumors about Detective Williams."

"Nice friend indeed," Gretchen murmured. "Would you say he's shy?"

The officer shook her head. "Oh no. He's a real nice guy, but he's just private. There are several women on the force who would love to date him. He'd be a great catch."

"Alvarez," the other officer shouted.

The police woman touched Gretchen's arm. "It was great seeing you, but I need to get back to work."

"You too, dear. Tell your father hello," Gretchen yelled after her. "So, he's private. He'd be a great catch. Yes, he would if someone was fishing for men who only kiss you like there's no tomorrow, leave you breathless, and hightail it down to a crime scene. What are you about, Detective Williams?"

Gretchen turned away from the murder site and headed to one of her favorite shops. It was way past time for therapy. As she entered the store, she spied a glorious pair of heels. They were brown leather with a black embroidered swirl along the side. They would go beautifully with…a new outfit. By the time she reached home several hours later, Daniel still hadn't called.

After a dinner of leftovers, she took a glass of wine and her cell phone to the balcony.

Gretchen stared at the phone. "Do something. Ring, buzz, or vibrate." *I want this stupid phone to ring.*

When the phone buzzed she nearly dropped it over the balcony's wall. Gretchen took a deep breath. "Hello."

"What time would you like me to pick you up tomorrow?"

Finally, Daniel. "I love to get to the park to watch batting practice."

"Really? I do too. I'll be at your place by eleven in the morning. Is that good?"

"More than good."

There was a pause on the other side of the discussion. "Good, great. I'll see you tomorrow. Goodnight." Click.

"What? That's it? Detective? Daniel?" Gretchen stood up and stamped her foot. "Why do I like you?"

Fine, Daniel. You've met your match, and I'll prove it to you. There won't be just home runs on that field tomorrow. I'm a great catch too.

As Gretchen plopped back down in her chair, her thoughts turned surprisingly to Chance. He had reentered her life so briefly over the summer after a lifetime of separation. Yet, he left her again, this time to welcome a grandchild. She still loved him, but it wasn't enough. She needed to be **in love** too.

The detective was prompt the next morning. Gretchen donned a tan pair of slim capris with an animal print sheer tunic. A light gold tank shimmered beneath. She finished off her look with several gold chains hanging around her neck, dripping down her chest. She wore her new pair of heels. A pair of gold bangle earrings hung beneath wisps of hair, while the rest was slicked back into a loose bun. She felt like a million dollars. She'd show her date what a real catch she was.

Williams dressed in dark washed jeans with a classic light blue button-down shirt. He had the sleeves rolled up, offering Gretchen a look at his tanned forearms. The detective wore no jewelry, not even a class ring. And Gretchen noticed months ago that any tan line from a wedding ring had long since faded. He wore simple brown loafers and was sockless. His hair was a little tousled for him, and he hadn't shaved for the day. Gretchen wasn't sure if she liked this Daniel. Her clean shaved and perfectly coiffed detective was more her style.

Before the game, Gretchen began to think she had made a serious miscalculation. Seldom did she read a person incorrectly, but the tentative, rather boring detective wasn't the best date she'd ever had. He wasn't even in the top fifty, or maybe even one hundred…She forced every laugh at his very few jokes. They sat in silence most of the time.

"Would you like something to drink?"

"He speaks," Gretchen said out loud. She had meant it to be an internal conversation, but she was mistaken. *Is this my day to make mistakes over and over?*

The detective seemed confused. "I thought you were concentrating on batting practice."

Gretchen pointed at the field. "They don't even concentrate most of the time. I was being quiet because you were."

Daniel Williams shut his eyes. When he opened them, a face bathed in disgust glared at him. "Really? I'm sorry, Ms. Malloy. Gretchen, sorry. Let's start over. Would you like a beer?"

"I would love one. Thank you." Gretchen smiled sweetly. "And if you could possibly add a hot dog to my order, that would be lovely."

"Well, you are easy."

Gretchen winked. "I have been told that before, and I'm not offended."

Daniel bowed his head. "Gretchen, you seem to forget that I know how difficult you can be. I tried to arrest you several times."

"But, dear detective, I would've needed to be guilty of something. I'm only guilty of being one of the most fascinating women you've ever met, and perhaps the best looking in handcuffs."

The detective surrendered. He flashed a quick smile before standing. "And I'm sure you're very familiar with many different styles of cuffs. I'll be right back. Anything on the hot dog?"

"Just mustard and relish."

With her companion away, Gretchen surveyed the stadium. She noticed a few familiar faces, and she waved to a couple of retired professional baseball players. They waved back, and one even blew her a kiss. Her attention returned to the field as the team's mascot ran bases with a few children.

Maybe I've moved too quickly with the man? He certainly takes his time. Now, I'm bored. If I could just ask him about the boy who was killed, we would have something in common again. Murder does that, doesn't it?

A hot dog appeared under her nose. "The lady asked for mustard and relish, and mustard and relish is what she receives."

"Thank you, Daniel. It is perfect."

"And two beers from my favorite brewery."

While they ate their ballpark cuisine, silence overtook them once more. The singing of the anthem occupied more time, followed by the first pitch of the game. It was the bottom of the first inning before Daniel commented on who his favorite player was.

"That guy always manages to make it on the bases."

Gretchen folded her arms over her ample chest. "Lucky for him. I wouldn't mind having someone make it to first base."

Williams heard the tone and smirked. "I bet you wouldn't mind someone sliding into second, or even going hard into third."

"Depending on his stamina or interest level, that might be interesting. If he isn't serious about the sport, he'll never hit a homerun. Besides, practice makes perfect."

Her companion shifted in his seat until his arm overlapped on her shoulder. He leaned in closely. "Are we still talking about the game or the other night?"

"I refuse to answer on the grounds that it may incriminate me."

Williams gathered his thoughts, an activity he'd been doing quite frequently since meeting his companion. Truthfully, she was in his thoughts constantly when he wasn't wondering how and why Tito had been murdered.

"The pitch is to you. I usually ask a woman what she likes, what she wants, and how she wants it. I can serve up a homerun anytime, Ms. Malloy."

Holy Moly. Did it just get warmer? I'm not having a hot flash. Those days are way behind me. But his breath on my cheek, his arm around my shoulders, his thumb rubbing the tender part of my arm, and the light cologne blending with mine…Gretchen! "You do, do you? Well, I enjoy a good time with a man when he knows what he wants. Frequency and speed can be debated. I'm serving the pitch up to you, Daniel."

Williams moved ever closer to the woman beside him. He made sure his leg was touching hers. There wasn't an inch of space, and he knew for certain he would carry her fragrance on his sleeve long after he departed her side later in the day. "Gretchen, you have to understand. I'm a long ball hitter, and I prefer to enjoy the game for all nine innings. What's the fun in a blow out in the first or second, when you can speculate way into the eighth who will win, or even who will score the most runs?"

Gretchen emitted a noise mimicking a huff, topped with a puff. She mulled his analogy over in her head. "I plan on winning, Detective Williams."

Williams laughed. "Do you? Well, I don't plan on striking out so I guess we have a game."

Gretchen shoved his arm. "Drink your beer. Oh, I'll need popcorn and peanuts in a bit." *And I need you to leave so I can cool off.*

"You are very needy, aren't you?"

"I prefer the term high maintenance, and it is well deserved. One must tend to a garden to keep it beautiful and blooming."

The player at home plate struck a ball that kept flying, heading toward the fountains.

"That's a homerun," Daniel yelled as he stood. Gretchen joined him, touching his arm in celebration. Finally, the tension had passed.

"He's a much better DH than an outfielder," Gretchen analyzed.

"You know what a designated hitter is?"

"Of course, Daniel. I know baseball, and the men who play the game."

Daniel shook his head. *Of course you do.* "Would I get points if I told you I was scouted by the majors?"

Gretchen gave him a once-over review. "You would get points. What position did you play?"

"Utility, but I loved catching."

Gretchen's breathing stopped briefly. *Be still my heart.* She glanced at her detective once more. *Yes, now I see he has the body of a catcher. His broad shoulders, muscular forearms, his tight upper legs, and when he walks away...*

"I do love a catcher. They're in charge, and in my personal opinion, they have the best physiques."

Daniel took a generous drink from his beer. *Is the sun beating right down on us?* "You do have to be in shape to play that position."

Are we still talking about the game? "Daniel, I'm not one for waiting. As you know, I say what I want to say."

"Yes, you do," Daniel quickly agreed.

"Well then, I need to know something, but for once in my life I'm terribly confused. I don't want to watch this entire game in complete confusion as we intellectually spar with witty repartee and innuendo. You are very good at it, by the way."

"Gretchen, just spit it out." Daniel pointed toward the pitcher. "Did you see that? I think he balked."

Gretchen, despite her discomfort, did see the infraction. "I did. He did. Hey, umps, we all saw a balk. Are you sleeping? Have you been paid off?"

Daniel attempted to stifle his laughter as he sheepishly looked up at his now standing date. The premier planner began to entice others in the crowd to voice their opinions. Another pitch was thrown, yet there was still no call. Gretchen had their entire section standing in protest. The hometown coach called a timeout and walked slowly over to home plate.

A revolt began in the stands as the beloved coach argued with the umpire, pointed at the pitcher, shook his head in disgust, and finally kicked dirt on the man. The umpire raised his arm signaling the ejection of the coach. Daniel stood next to the woman who had begun it all.

He smiled as Gretchen let out one of the loudest whistles he'd ever heard. The woman had a variety of talents, many of them he feared. "That umpire is looking right up at you."

"Good." Gretchen pointed toward the man. "You stink. Yeah, you! I'm watching you."

The umpire shook a finger toward her way as Daniel forced her to sit down. "That's enough, Joan of Arc."

"My, that was fun, but I prefer to think of myself as a modern-day woman. We will not shut me up in the face of injustice." Gretchen elbowed him in his side. "I think I need snacks."

"I'll be right back. Please don't get yourself in trouble while I'm away."

Gretchen winked. "Do you know me?"

Moments later the detective returned with popcorn and a bag of peanuts. "You bought both? How kind. What will you be eating?"

"I thought we'd share."

Gretchen smiled. "Do you believe we are at that point in our relationship?"

"I was hoping we'd share. It's just popcorn."

"Popcorn is a metaphor for so many things," she said as she dug her hand into the box. "It's still warm." Gretchen ate a few pieces and stuck her hand in again. This time, Daniel's hand touched hers. She looked up at him. "See? A metaphor. I can choose to share on–"

"Sharing can be much more enjoyable."

Gretchen's heart skipped a beat. It was the tone in his voice, deep and sweet. It was the look in his eyes, hot and yet cool. *My, my, what is with this man?* "Daniel, we broached this subject the other night, but do you have a problem with my age?"

He looked into her eyes, smiled, and then removed his hand full with popcorn. "Do you have a problem with mine?"

"Of course not. I've been with much younger men."

The detective shrugged. "I'm not sure if that's good or bad for me. Has this age thing been bothering you? Is that why you're not acting like yourself?"

"I'm acting like me," Gretchen huffed. "You're the one who seems to be different." *And who went to a crime scene, and apparently has his secrets.*

"Am not."

"I thought that was you sitting down here." Hal's voice drew attention. Gretchen's old friend, and mayor of the city was standing next to her. He glanced over at her companion. "Detective, what a pleasant surprise."

Williams stood up instantly, but Hal waved him off as he sat down next to Gretchen. "Why aren't you up at the club level?"

"I like sitting closer to the game, besides the club is wonderful for networking. Is your lovely wife with you?"

"Nope. She's with our daughter at the high school. Have you talked to Marty? How is his senate campaign?"

Gretchen hadn't talked to her dear friend Marty since the day she took Chance to the airport. It had only been a few days, but it seemed forever. "I'll call him tomorrow. I believe he's in Springfield today for a speech."

"Good. I'm happy you talked him into staying in the fight." Hal bent around Gretchen. "By the way, Williams, you did some fine work on that murder case."

Daniel retained his gaze on the field. "Thank you. Ms. Malloy did help quite a bit. She was relentless."

Playfully, she nudged him. "You couldn't have done it without me, right?"

"Right." Daniel's eyes never left the game.

Gretchen turned her attention to Hal. "He's a man of few words. We should have lunch soon, Hal."

"No, you should come over for dinner. I'll talk to my wife, and we will set a date." He lowered his head to whisper. "You could bring the detective if you want."

"Thank you, but we're just friends." She could barely spit out the word. It left a bad taste in her mouth, yet it seemed she needed to explain their relationship. "Text or call me. It would be wonderful to catch up."

"And you could tell me how you caught the killer. Everyone is talking about it. I better get back. Talk soon. Goodbye, Williams."

Daniel stood up out of respect. Gretchen glared. "Sit down, Daniel. He isn't the president or the pope. I think I've figured out your problem. You're mad because everyone is saying I caught the killer."

He did as he was instructed and sat down. "Don't be ridiculous. Not everyone is talking about it." He paused. "Just the whole blasted department and the news media."

"How delightful." Gretchen's face lit up like the sun until she looked over at the man next to her. "Oh. They're making fun of you."

"I can take it, Gretchen. I can take it for a few hours. After an entire day, it gets a little old. Frankly, we had such a good night. I guess I've been a bit off of my game." *And a kid who had such great promise is dead.*

Gretchen rolled her eyes. "Are we back to the game? I was happy to help with your case, and I needed to clear my name. I was interfering, irritating, and I'm sure obnoxious at times, but it all worked out in the end. Didn't it?"

"It was unexpected." Daniel grabbed another handful of popcorn.

Gretchen touched his hand. "I can always help, Daniel. If you have a problem with a case, I would be there for you."

Daniel nodded but needed to change the subject. "I've been meaning to ask you something."

A base hit became a double. Gretchen clapped. "Anything, detective. It's not like you haven't questioned me before now."

Daniel pointed down at her shoes. "Do you always wear heels?"

"Not always," Gretchen answered shyly. She batted her lush, fake eyelashes. "I don't wear them in bed."

"I'd have to see that to believe it." Daniel chewed and smiled at the same time. "I believe in verification." He winked at her as though he was a young boy with a frog behind his back.

Two can play. "Anytime, Daniel. Feel free to see for yourself, friend."

Daniel's laugh filled the air. "You are outrageous. No wonder I thought you killed that groom. I'm beginning to think Chance got out within an inch of his life, and I may be in jeopardy. I've had a good life."

Gretchen playfully elbowed him. "But it'll be better with me in it."

Daniel took her hand in his. "It's been a good game. Let's get out of here and get something real to eat." He didn't give her time to answer as he stood and pulled her up with him.

Gretchen, for once, willingly did as she was told and followed. *Maybe I do like this Daniel?*

Chapter Four

"Detective," the server at the Italian restaurant yelled as he arrived at their table.

"How are you, Tommy?"

The man handed a large menu to Daniel. "And for the pretty lady," he added as he offered Gretchen hers. "Dad is visiting his sister in Miami. It's good he's finally taking a break."

"Good for him."

Gretchen squinted at the menu as the two men caught up. *I can't see anything without those readers anymore, but I don't want to look…I refuse to say the word!* She could just order lasagna, and her companion wouldn't realize anything. *This candlelight makes me look fabulous. I don't want to ruin the mood.*

Gretchen looked up over the menu when she heard the silence. Daniel was staring at her.

"I do know you can't read a darn thing on that menu, don't you?"

Gretchen waved him off. "What are you talking about?"

The detective gave her a side glance. "Read me the salads you might like."

He placed his own menu on the table and crossed his arms in front of his chest to challenge her. Gretchen squinted. She couldn't find the salads if she had to pick one to feed a bunny. She dropped the menu soundly on the table and stuck her tongue out in his direction.

"Fine, smarty."

Williams chuckled. "Gretchen, just get your glasses out. No one will think less of you."

I will. One to not wallow in self-pity and always up to a challenge, Gretchen dug into her purse and resurrected the much-needed readers. She defiantly positioned them on her nose and began to look over the plentiful choices. "At least my glasses are stylish." The purple frames featured gold specks and a swirl on the nosepiece.

"You know, you kind of look like a naughty school marm with those on."

Gretchen's eyes widened. "What?" She caught her breath as she met his eyes. *Why is he always keeping me off balance? There's times I almost fall off my heels when I'm around him.*

"You heard me," Daniel murmured. "I think they're sexy."

Gretchen removed the glasses and leaned across the table. "You're a strange one, detective."

"I prefer to think that I'm unique. You have me intrigued."

"Ah. So what should I order? You apparently are a fixture here."

Daniel nodded. "You could say that. Tommy was in some trouble a few years ago, and I helped him out. I've known his dad since I came to Kansas City, and I was searching for authentic Italian food."

Gretchen was dismayed that as a woman who knew everyone in the city, she knew nothing of her detective. "Where did you come from?"

"I'm originally from the east coast, but I've lived in so many places. The eggplant is very good. The chicken spiedini is amazing, but it's a little spicy."

Gretchen studied him as he continued to read the food items. His eyes were soft. His hair was graying around the edges of his face, pulling the color from his eyes as though they were prized jewels. Even when he thought she was a killer, he had never creased his brow or snarled at her as though she was the worst person on the face of the earth. *How could he think that of me? I'm wonderful.*

"Daniel, I usually do not surrender this much power to a man, but please order for me. I want to see what you think I'd like."

Daniel clapped his hands. "Wonderful! You're going to love the food."

Gretchen giggled at his wide smile. "You seem very confident."

He nodded. "I am." He winked. "If nothing else, I am confident."

Daniel ordered and soon their table was filled with wine, bread, and a tray of antipasto. Tommy, his hands on his hips, seemed overly happy.

"Dad is going to be so happy to hear you finally brought a lady here."

Daniel shoved a piece of warm bread dipped into an oil mixture in front of Gretchen's face. "Here. Try this."

Gretchen motioned her head in the direction of Tommy. "He's still standing there, and he's just smiling."

Daniel glared at the happy server. "Don't you have somewhere to go?"

Tommy scampered away quickly as Gretchen filled her mouth with the tasty bread. "This is very good. So, you've only come in here alone?"

Daniel savored a sip from his glass of wine. "I go alone to most places."

"Are you happy with that, or are you atoning for some past indiscretion?" Gretchen dug her fork into the salad and plucked out a piece of artichoke.

"I'm fine with my own company."

"And the indiscretion?" Gretchen chided him but added a smile. "You know I love that sort of activity."

Daniel's tone changed quickly. "I have a few I'd rather not talk about."

Gretchen realized immediately that she had crossed a line. With Lily, Abby, and even with some of her clients, she frequently walked metaphorically too far off the diving board, but she was trying to change her ways. "I'm sorry. I didn't mean anything by what I said. I suppose we don't know each other that well, even though we did solve that case together."

Daniel stabbed at a piece of lettuce. "Ah, the case. I believe I did all the paperwork."

"And I received all the glory. Isn't that the way it's supposed to be when you're working with a local celebrity like me?"

"You do draw attention from police, mayors, disgruntled umpires, men in general–"

Gretchen purred. "Like bees to honey, and I'm the queen bee!"

Daniel's brows creased. "That didn't sound right, but I do love honey."

"Have you ever licked it off–"

Daniel reached across the table to gather her hand in his. "Stop. Please don't ruin the moment with some salacious story about you and some other man."

Gretchen's hand was on fire. She opened her mouth to speak, to have words flow off of her sharp tongue. Usually, verbiage fell out into the air like confetti dripping from a New Year's Eve ball. She enjoyed hearing herself speak, but this time she looked down at the large, soft hand enveloping hers and remained silent. She was consumed by his warmth. For once, Gretchen Malloy kept her mouth shut. *This man is a wizard.*

After an amazing meal, the couple sipped their coffee. Gretchen leaned back in her chair. "I haven't had a meal like that since, well, I don't really recall. I'm so used to takeout and expensive event dinners that I'd forgotten how good homemade Italian food can be. I'm so full I'm not sure I can breathe."

"I'm happy you enjoy this special place." Daniel waved at Tommy to bring the check. He had an early Monday morning and needed to call it a night.

Tommy stood next to the table. "Detective, could you come to the counter to pay? We've had some security issues."

"Sure. Gretchen, I'll be right back, and then I'll get you home."

Smiling sweetly was painful for Gretchen. *How does Lily do it? She's probably the nicest person I know, but even she has a little mean streak when it comes to her husband, or if she's hungry.* It was more than a few minutes before Daniel came back to her. He said very little as they left the restaurant.

Gretchen finally broached the silence. "Is everything okay?"

"Um, sure. Tommy had some news for me."

"Of the criminal variety?"

Daniel shook his head. "You don't stop, do you? Do you see a mystery in every corner of this city?"

"Perhaps, because there is a mystery everywhere. My friend Lily can find one in a box of flowers. I can discover one at a wedding. Daniel, you're the mystery."

Daniel smiled. "And you are an enigma."

Gretchen began to wind a wisp of her hair with her finger. "Do you like enigmas?"

"On a good day, I think they are amazing. When they give me a headache, I find them completely irritating."

"Daniel, after today, I've been wondering. Why exactly did you come to my apartment the other day?"

"Even though you are the queen of glam, you certainly can be direct." Daniel sighed. "I admire your passion. You have passion for your friends, clothes, makeup, and even those damn heels. I couldn't believe it, but I wanted to know you."

"My, that's not much of a compliment, Daniel." Gretchen gazed out her passenger window. To her surprise, she flicked away a tear from her right eye. *I'm crying because of an eyelash. I'm certain of it.*

"You do know that you can rub people the wrong way, right? I mean, you gave me instant headaches, and then I couldn't get you out of my head. Besides, when Chance left–"

"What?" Gretchen yelled. "Did you think I would be so lonely that I'd just roll over–"

"Stop. No. I thought you might be upset. I thought maybe–"

"You would comfort the poor old lady? You'd keep her company while the man was away? My bed is never that cold, buddy."

Daniel rubbed his left temple. "My headache is returning. Will you just listen to me for a second?"

Gretchen huffed. "I'll give you one minute, and then you never have to see me again. I'll be moving into the senior facility in just a few weeks."

"Now, that I would love to see. I can picture you clicking down the hallways in those heels. Two or three old farts would die at the mere sight of you. Their hearts wouldn't be able to take it. God forbid you'd wear that tight little number you wore the night I caught you in the dumpster looking for evidence."

Gretchen pretended to smooth her hair. "That outfit was burned. People can be such pigs. I can still feel those catsup packages bursting under my feet."

"Gretchen, I came by that day because," Daniel paused. Stopped at a traffic light, he glanced over to see her face. Even in the darkness, she appeared to glow with life. "Because, I missed you. And yes, because you were available. I don't give a hoot about age. I care about getting to know you, and I waited until Chance stepped aside. He's a great man. I know you two were very close."

As the light turned green, Daniel returned his attention to his driving. This wasn't going well for him. How could he tell her that despite his better judgment, he was drawn to her? The silence in the vehicle was unforgiving. He quickly turned the car into a vacant parking lot just a few blocks from her apartment. He turned the car off and stared ahead.

"Your GPS is off. My apartment is down the street. I could walk from here."

He could hear the disdain in her voice. And her anger. Daniel freed himself from the seatbelt so he could turn to her. He placed his arm across the back of her seat.

"Gretchen, I want to get to know you. You are vibrant, insanely energetic, and unrelenting. You are one of the most honest people I've ever met. But you are also a real pain in the neck. I'm sure I'm not the first person to tell you that. I haven't gone out with a real woman in a very long time. You are a real woman, and that's who I want."

Before Gretchen could protest, her open mouth was closed with those amazing heat-inflicting lips. Daniel moved his arm to her shoulders and pulled her closer. With his other hand he held her face, the thumb rubbing away a line of tears. When he finally pulled away, he massaged her neck. "Well, Ms. Malloy?"

Gretchen slowly opened her eyes and licked her lips. "Well, well, detective."

"No more doubts? No more age comments? No more headaches for me?" Daniel patted her shoulder and reconnected his seat belt. He started the engine, pulled back onto the street, and briefly looked over at her. She remained silent. Gretchen Malloy was silent. Someone should alert the media.

When he pulled the car into the apartment's drive, she remained motionless in the car. As he came to her side to open her door, he waved off the night valet. Gretchen slipped out of the car in one fluid movement. She stood only inches from him.

"I've been told what you want, Daniel. Now, what will you give me?" Gretchen asked. With her heels, she stood eye-to-eye with him.

He searched her eyes. One side of his mouth lifted in a quirky smile. "I'll give you a good run for your money."

Gretchen attempted to remain emotionless, but it grew more difficult when staring into those pools of heaven. "Well then." Placing her hands on either side of his face she whispered, "Daniel, I can run in these shoes, and I never lose."

"I'm counting on that." He laced his hands behind her back, capturing her in a strong embrace.

"Goodnight, Daniel." Gretchen garnered every bit of energy from the tip of her stilettos to plant a kiss on his lips. Her intention was to leave a red imprint so he would see it when he brushed his teeth tonight. When she attempted to pull away, he melded her body to his for one final kiss that left a mark on her, one that made her heart beat faster than it had in years.

"Goodnight, Gretchen."

Daniel released her. He winked before he got into his car and drove away. Gretchen's right ankle gave away. She nearly fell as her heel betrayed her. "That man! He's going to kill me."

She was comforted that he hadn't seen her lose her balance again, but he had. As the detective grabbed one more look of her from his rearview mirror, he saw her stumble. He didn't want to laugh, but he did, loudly as he headed home. From what he heard about her from the mayor, the police chief, her friend running for the senate, and even from Chance, Gretchen was a superhero. Insults bounced off of her, but when she was around him, she weakened.

"I'm her kryptonite." *I haven't had this much fun in years.* But she could read him like a book, and that left a very uncomfortable feeling in his stomach. He'd held his secrets for so long he wasn't sure he could live in the light of truth ever again.

Chapter Five

"Gretchen, it's Daniel. I need some information."

"Happy Monday to you too." Gretchen was on her second cup of coffee. She didn't do Mondays, well at least not until ten in the morning. She always woke early, but she just couldn't seem to move today. *Are those kisses zapping me of my super-powers?*

The detective chuckled. "Yes, good morning. How are you?"

"As always, I'm fabulous. What do you need? I have everything you might need."

Daniel cleared his throat. "I wondered if you knew anything about a high-end store that is reopening on the Plaza?"

"Yes, of course. I'm planning Laurent's grand re-opening. Their New York corporate offices refurbished all four floors. You know, I've always wanted to see their store in Paris. I hear they have circus performers hanging in the air. Can you imagine shopping for a new pair of heels while a trapeze artist is above you? Now that's high fashion. Get it?"

Daniel rolled his eyes. He had made a mistake calling her this early on a Monday, at least it was for him. "Yes. They're having a big party, right?"

"I'm planning it so it will be the event of the season. What do you need to know?"

"I need a guest list, vendor information–"

"Don't forget the entertainers. We're featuring an aerial group."

"Wonderful, Gretchen. I need names from valets to custodians. Can you do that for me?"

Luckily, the detective couldn't see the planner bouncing up and down on her couch. Sheer delight coursed through her veins. *Another mystery is afoot.* "Of course, but I need to know why."

"No, you really don't."

Gretchen lounged back. "Yes, I really do if you want that information."

Daniel leaned back in his chair. He waved at the lead detective on Tito's case. The man was headed into the conference room. "Gretchen, there was a murder the other night."

"Yes, and you knew the boy who was killed."

Daniel sprung to a standing position. "How did you know that? Never mind, you know everything in this city."

"I do, including that you knew him, and you thought he was a good kid. You are a good judge of people, unless you're charging a stunningly beautiful woman of murder. Then, your judgment is just plain awful."

At the door of the conference room, Beckham was waving for him. "We can discuss my judgment later. In fact,

I'm wondering about it myself. But what if you give me the lists, and I'll bring you dinner tonight?"

"Food pro quo? I like it. Don't come before six. I have a meeting at the club for a New Year's Eve party we're planning."

"I have to go. See you after six." Click.

"Why does he do that? I never get a chance to say goodbye." *Hmm, he never allows me to say goodbye?*

It was nearly half past six when Gretchen buzzed the detective up that evening. Attired in skin-tight leather capris, a black mock turtleneck, and a flowing flowered kimono Gretchen leaned against the open door seductively as she waited for the elevator door to open.

When Daniel was revealed, he was tugging at his tie. The brown bag he carried was colored by a huge grease stain. "Hello beautiful." He said it before he actually looked at her. Once he did, he did a double take. *That's similar to her dumpster diving outfit that night.* He nonchalantly strode past her until he reached the kitchen and removed the styrofoam boxes.

Gretchen stomped a heel on the wood floor. "Excuse me. I'm standing here like a goddess. A little attention is necessary."

Daniel looked up as he licked his finger. Barbecue sauce oozed out onto Gretchen's marble countertop. "I said hello. I brought the best. You like ribs, right?"

Daniel reached for a towel to clean his hand as he came around the counter. "About that. You don't need to do all of this. You could wear a bag and look like you just walked down the runway in a fashion show."

He was close enough that Gretchen felt his warm breath on her neck. She felt her face warm. "I need to change. This outfit is dry clean only, and I'm not about to eat ribs while wearing it. There's beer and wine in the fridge."

Gretchen left her guest standing in the middle of her living room. He shrugged and strode to the refrigerator. By the time she returned, Daniel had the meal set out and was drinking his favorite beer. Gretchen found her wine bottle and poured herself a full glass. "Are your parents still alive?"

Her question came out of the blue. "My father passed away when I was in high school. My mother is alive." He began to fill a plate with ribs, baked beans, and coleslaw. He opened another container. "I knew the fries were in here."

"I'm sorry about your father. Are you close to your mother? Is she in good health?"

Daniel's mouth was full with a pickle spear. "I'm so hungry, aren't you?"

Gretchen took the cue, and there was no more talk of family as they ate. After they cleaned up, Gretchen pulled a folder from her bag and handed it off to Daniel. She sat next to him on the couch. "This is the guest list so far. These marks here are those who have responded. We'll be calling the others next week. I've attached the vendor contracts and certificates of insurance, the subcontractors such as the bartenders, etc. I gather they are having a special showing of rare red diamonds so our security will be heightened. Everyone at the event will be checked, with no exceptions."

Daniel shuffled through the papers. "What about the store's staff and security?"

Gretchen snuggled closer until their arms were touching. "I don't believe I have that."

"Can you get it without alarms going off?"

Gretchen pulled back. "Excuse me? Can I get it? I'm the best in this city, and one of the most elite planners in the nation. I can do anything, and no one will suspect me."

Daniel smiled. "I suspected you. I found you in that dumpster. I figured you would show up at the victim's parents' home. Do you want me to continue?"

Gretchen kissed his cheek. "You're special."

Daniel read through another page. "Gretchen, do they say where the diamonds are coming from?"

"That should be on the vendor list. It's a company out of New York, RW Diamonds and Stones. Is all of this connected to your friend's death?"

Daniel ignored her question as he ran his finger down the list of names and companies. He pointed at one name in particular. "The Hamptons are one of the sponsors? Their son was just killed in June."

"Yes, it does seem unusual, but they were sponsors way before he was killed at my wedding by Marty's crazy wife. They aren't paying for anything. They just have their names attached to bring in other big money for the charity. The ladies at the club were just talking about them. At least they aren't linking me to the scandal."

Daniel patted her leg. "Have they been nice to you since you cracked the case?"

Gretchen waved her hand. "Oh please. They don't care. That scandal has passed. They only care about today, and what ivy league school their children or grandchildren will attend."

"Why are people still impressed with those schools?"

Gretchen was shocked. "Because, dear Daniel, they are the best."

"It depends."

"You're in a mood. I'm surprised you're so judgmental. I think you're grieving."

Daniel rose up from the couch quickly. "I can't afford to grieve, Gretchen." His dark look faded as quickly as it had flared up. He waved the file in the air. "Thanks for doing this. I need to go."

If Gretchen had been standing, he would've bowled her over with his behavior. "What? You're going?"

"I've had a long day, and I have an even longer week. Maybe we can see each other this weekend again?" He grabbed his necktie and began a trail of retreat to the door.

"I'll be coordinating a wedding, so I'll be busy from Thursday until Sunday afternoon." Gretchen slowly made her way to the door, disappointment in every step.

Daniel opened the door. "Okay, well maybe we can plan something the week after. Thanks again."

"Daniel." Gretchen stood alone in the doorway as he hit the elevator button to go down. Her ankle turned, but before she lost her balance, she kicked off both heels. She began to close the door when a hand broke her movement.

"I forgot something."

Gretchen's left brow arched. "What? The leftovers? Do you want a beer for the road?"

"No, this," he whispered. He lowered his head until he captured her lips. He kissed her senseless, moving his lips from her top to bottom lip, then taking her wholly. Her arms were useless at her sides. Embraced by only his one arm, Gretchen was entangled and captured. Literally and figuratively. She truly had never met anyone like him.

As he began to leave, he kissed the top of her head. "Without those heels, I tower over you, like you might actually need me. But we both know you don't. That kiss might hold you until I see you again. Keep the leftovers, beautiful."

This time, Daniel left and didn't return. His thoughts needed to be on tomorrow and a phone call to a DEA agent who might be able to help him.

Gretchen drew in a full breath, picked up her heels, then cleaned up the kitchen, and headed to the bathroom for a very, very long cold shower.

Chapter Six

"Tom Fullerton from the FBI suggested I contact you," Detective Williams admitted as he spoke to the DEA agent on the other end of the phone. He shuffled two folders on his desk. We just had a second murder here involving two young men I knew. One was an informer for our gang unit. He was the first body drop and was basically beaten to death. The second was found in the same area. He was apparently forced to take a drug. We're still testing, but it seems to be synthetic fentanyl mixed with something. I hear you're an expert in this sort of thing. I'm concerned this is becoming a trend in Kansas City."

Devlin Pierce, miles away in Virginia, was surprised to hear a familiar name and place from the police detective. "Tom thought you and I would get along. He sent me a text yesterday about this. Were you close to the men?"

Williams shut his eyes briefly. Tito had been such a success story. Daniel had originally met him through a boxing program for youth. They used to spar every Thursday night, only after Tito finished his homework. Daniel had tutored the boy through algebra. The young man was on his way out of the dangerous world he grew up in.

He was still grieving Tito's death, when he was called by RJ's mother the other night. Her youngest son hadn't returned home from his job at the local grocery store. It was almost two in the morning. By the time the detective asked a couple of patrol cars to search the neighborhood, it was almost daylight. A member of the construction crew had arrived early behind the posh department store where Gretchen was having her future event. He found RJ's body dumped at the other end of the same alley where Tito had been discovered.

"I steered the first young man onto a better path, but our latest victim was very special to me. He was clean. His mother made sure her boys were kept out of trouble. She even moved the family every two years so the boys wouldn't be involved in the gangs. Her oldest is a junior in college, and he's there on full athletic and academic scholarships."

Dev could hear the anguish in the detective's voice. He personally knew that pit-of-the-stomach feeling when you found a child dead, but two in a short span of time would gut the strongest individual. "I'm sorry, Williams. You are sure neither one was involved in drugs or in gangs?"

"Absolutely, Agent Pierce. After I spoke to Agent Fullerton, I met with the local DEA. They looked over both cases. Tito, the first young man, had plans to join the FBI. RJ would never take drugs, sell drugs, or participate in a gang. The DEA says they've been focusing on a group transporting synthetic drugs throughout the state. I also received some information from one of my own informants about a high-end simulated drug coming through Kansas City. I didn't catch Tito's case. All I can concentrate on is RJ's murder. Maybe they saw something? Maybe they knew something? Tito wanted to talk to me. I would've seen RJ tonight. There were missed chances."

"Could you send me those files, and the notes you have from either case, or even from your informant? I'll take a look. I just returned from the border where we were working on fentanyl being shipped through Texas straight up Interstate 35 to Kansas City. It all could be related and your kids just got in the way."

Williams drummed his fingers on his desk. "Agent Pierce, it's too coincidental that they were both found in a high rent area, behind a store that's being refurbished. No one is around that store at night except for security. I'm tracking down the private company now. Something isn't right. I'm hearing a buzz, and I'm worried. This place is having a large grand opening charity event in just a few weeks. It doesn't need any more trouble there. And no one else needs to die."

Dev began to scribble down a few notes. "I'm familiar with Kansas City. Where is the store?"

"Down on the Plaza. It's a large outdoor shopping center–"

Dev chuckled. "Oh, I know it very well. I was married in your city, and our reception was held only blocks from that site. Tell me the buzz you've heard…"

For another hour the two law enforcement officers traded information and speculated.

"What is gnawing at me is a few details not everyone knows. You see, I'm a real nerd on patterns. There's one that is of a particular interest of mine, a personal interest."

Dev Pierce looked out his window. He could sometimes be a nerd too, and patterns were always an interest of his. "I completely understand. What is it?"

"My family has an interest in diamonds. I've been researching our courier routes, and I've discovered an unusual anomaly. Maybe it's nothing, but once our pouches are delivered to a high-end store for a special sale or event, there seems to be a surge in drug overdoses, mostly synthetic fentanyl hiding in pills. Our narcs always say that it was a recent delivery. I would hate to think that those deliveries are directly correlated, but after RJ's murder, I'm beginning to wonder. We've also been losing some of our inventory."

Dev sat up. "How so?" His occasional missions in the Cayman Islands made him remember how diamonds were used for overseas drug payments.

"Our couriers are checked over and over, but some pouches weigh less than when they were first packed. I'll send you some of the logs. Then, three years ago this store opened, and they're already refurbishing?"

Dev laughed. "You aren't married, are you?"

"No, I'm divorced."

"My wife has reorganized our bedroom closet three times. We moved into our home, and when she was pregnant all the clothes she might wear were moved to the lower hangers. So, when it comes to fashion, I really don't think it's that unusual. Since both bodies were dumped there, I'd almost say someone is sending a message to a contact there at the store, or even the construction company."

Williams mulled that thought over. He'd look over the personnel files again for the store and the construction company. "What if I told you that the grand opening is a charity event, and it will feature several rare diamonds from my family's company?"

"I'd say this event may be the perfect cover for a drug shipment, or even the heist of some very rare diamonds."

Williams shook his head. "Crap. Well, I was thinking that very same thing. Six months ago, our company supplied diamonds for a sale benefiting an art museum in Chicago. The event was held at a gallery. The night before, your DEA found cocaine in the back of a secure vehicle carrying our merchandise. When I say this stuff out loud it all sounds like a movie plot."

Dev hit a few computer keys to open the case file the detective was referencing. The agents had a shootout with the drivers, but the suspects disappeared down Michigan Avenue. There did seem to be something, but…

"Detective, give me a few days to look into this. Sometimes, reality is more bizarre than a movie, but it's just as dangerous. Don't underestimate your gut feeling. When is this event again?"

"A couple of weeks. I sent all my notes and information by email. I know a woman involved in the planning, and I'm trying to discover what I can without telling her of my suspicions."

Another agent walked into Dev's office. "Do you think she's involved?"

"No. She's just connected to everyone. She's friends with the mayor."

Dev Pierce signed off on a file the agent had dropped on his desk and then left the room. "So you're doing your own undercover work?"

"Agent Pierce, that would be unprofessional."

Suddenly, Dev realized the implication. "Sorry, Williams. I mean, you're investigating without her suspecting that you're doing it." Dev knew exactly what the detective was up against. Lily and he had met over a misdirected drug shipment. He'd suspected her briefly, but then found her more valuable for the information in her head, and her amazing ability to see things he didn't. Eventually, he'd even used her as bait to reel in a drug dealer. He continued to make up for that in any way he could on a daily basis.

"Yes. If she realizes what I'm up to, there'll be hell to pay." The DEA agent didn't need to know that Gretchen and he had met over a murder. He definitely didn't need to be aware of the few kisses they shared.

"I know women like that. My wife has this inhuman skill to know when I'm fibbing, even if it's about what I ate for lunch. I don't lie to her, but sometimes I just don't say anything. Even then, she swears she knows my 'tells'. Thankfully, she only uses her abilities for good."

"It seems the women we know are formidable."

"You have no idea, Williams. I'll look over your files and I'll do some digging on this end. If you can, forward your company's information and a little bit about the transport process. Thanks for checking in. I'll be in touch no matter what I find."

"Thanks, Agent Pierce. Maybe my business just has a problem, but if it could involve drugs, I'll shut down everything before I allow criminal activities to smear my family's name. Besides, I need to know what happened to my boys."

"Detective, there are times when I think I've seen everything, and just when I think I can't see anything new, some mule carries cocaine in their underwear, oatmeal, or even in a dead shark. You never know. Several years ago at the space center in Florida, which has zero tolerance on drugs, there was a bag of cocaine found outside of a restroom. If someone can leave it there with all of their security, they can move it anywhere."

"I understand. Thanks again, Agent Pierce."

Daniel Williams, feeling as though he was in over his head, felt some consolation. It seemed as if the DEA agent could be the cavalry rescue he desperately needed. The suspicions about the store, even Gretchen's event, could very well be the epicenter of something big. *She'll never forgive me if she finds out what I'm doing. Now, I need her to invite me to this blasted party.*

The rest of the week, at every turn, Williams hit a brick wall in his investigation. By Friday, he admitted to himself that he needed to hear Gretchen's voice. When all he could listen to was her phone message, he told her he was overwhelmed by a case and that he'd try calling her on Sunday. Tomorrow, he would attend a teenager's funeral. He would have to tell RJ's mother that they were doing everything they could to gain justice for her son's murder. Life would go on, but without RJ's smiling face greeting him Sunday morning at the center. He'd have to explain to those left behind why one of his favorite kids wasn't there. But they probably understood better than he did.

Chapter Seven

By Sunday afternoon, Daniel Williams found himself driving around the city. His vehicle made the path decision, and it decided to park in Gretchen's apartment building's driveway. The young man at the door came to his side and knocked on the window. Daniel was miles away in thought. Finally, he responded with a smile as he opened his car door. "Is Ms. Malloy in?"

"Yes, detective. I'll park your car for you. Go on up."

How did he know me? Of course! Gretchen probably told him. Daniel buzzed her apartment.

"Hello?"

"Gretchen, it's me. Are you still speaking to me after this week?"

"Come up, Daniel. Say absolutely nothing about anything. Is that understood?"

Daniel didn't know how to answer. But he said yes. He'd been instructed to always tell the diva planner yes, and he was discovering his life was just easier that way.

He walked slowly out of the elevator and noticed her front door ajar. He opened it slowly. "Gretchen, nothing illegal is going on, is it? Are you okay?"

"No criminal behavior, and yes, I'm fine."

He assumed her voice came from one of the bedrooms. "Is this a bad time?"

"Not really. I want you to know that when I was younger, probably up until last year, I used to wake up early to put makeup on before, well, before any gentleman visitor could see me. You can't laugh, and you must promise me you will never tell anyone what you're about to see."

Daniel came here for peace. Instead, he was more perplexed about the mysteries of the world. "You seem to forget I've seen your mugshot." He made her take that photo so he could use it for target practice when he first met her. She grew on him, sort of like mold on bread. But in the end, she was the penicillin, the medicine he needed. "I promise I won't divulge what I'm about to see."

Slowly, Gretchen peeked around the corner of the hallway. He noticed at first glance that she was shoeless. Instead of skin-tight leggings or a short skirt, she was wearing jeans. Her shirt was an old faded sweatshirt. She wasn't adorned with any jewelry, not even earrings. Her hair was down. When he saw her face, his jaw dropped. Gretchen didn't have one drop of makeup on and her eyelashes were natural.

"You are sickened by my face, aren't you?" She hurried into the kitchen and poured from the wine bottle on the counter. "I just arrived home an hour ago, and I was just pooped."

Daniel turned toward her but remained non-responsive. He followed her with his eyes. She was…

"I know. You can really see my age with all of the fairy dust removed. I shouldn't have let you in. I received your message Friday, but I was just too busy. I hope you had a lovely weekend."

"Oh, it was just lovely," he finally muttered. He continued to stare at her as though she was a valuable piece of art. "Gretchen, you look, you are beautiful. You're ageless."

"Right. You're very charming, detective." Gretchen slugged down the remainder of the liquid in her glass and poured another measure. "I'm beginning to think you don't get around many women if you think that. I've been wondering about you."

"Have you had dinner?"

Gretchen finished another gulp. "No, silly. I'm drinking. You wouldn't believe what I've been through. The ring bearer flushed the rings down the toilet. They gave the damn kid the real rings. Who does that? Idiots. Then, the groom's uncle thought I was his wife. The poor man has dementia, but every time I walked by him, he pinched my butt and began to tell me what he was going to do to me when we got home. I know kinky, but this man was on a different level of kink!"

As Gretchen rambled, she noticed that Daniel looked as though he had been hit by a car and had died at the scene. "So, detective, what did you do this weekend? Can you beat my stories?"

Daniel began to speak and stopped. Finally, as he sat down in one of her counter chairs he answered. "I went to a funeral for another murdered teenager. This one was very close to me. He was such a great kid."

Now Gretchen understood why his eyes were dark and brooding. She saw the news coverage of a second body discovered in the same alley. "Oh, Daniel. I'm so sorry. Are you going to solve his murder? Of course you are. Is this one connected to the other? How did you know him? How close were you?" Gretchen abruptly shut her mouth. "I'm sorry. I'm so sorry."

For the woman who knew everyone and knew what to do in virtually every situation, Gretchen was in new territory. She reached for a beer in the refrigerator and placed the opened bottle in front of him. She received a slight smile for her effort. *What can I do to relieve his pain?*

The detective gazed at the bottle while Gretchen slowly walked around the island. She began to reach around his back, but he quickly turned into her arms. His head fell onto her shoulder, his lips nuzzling her neck. Gretchen held him. She remained silent. She slid her fingers through his hair, comforting him. She wasn't thinking of anything else but his pain. This was a new experience for the woman who enjoyed a one night stand and then moved on. *Am I getting old? No, it's because of him. Not only does he keep me off balance, he is changing my entire disposition. And I don't mind.*

He kissed her cheek as he pulled out of the intimate embrace. "Thank you."

She marveled at his sincerity. He wiped his eyes. There was no shame in tears. She had watched her father cry. He had been a strong, caring man, and he would think that Daniel was a good man.

Gretchen patted his arm. "Now, let's check my takeout menus and get us dinner."

Daniel wiped his eyes one more time. "What? You're not going to cook for me?" He winked. Already, he was feeling a little lighter.

"Oh, heaven's no, Daniel. You'll soon learn that I'm a magician, but the best trick I have in my repertoire is to place my finger on the phone, call a restaurant, and order food. It magically appears within twenty to thirty minutes. Then, you clap." Gretchen curtsied as though she was responding to a sold out audience.

Daniel clapped his hands. "Bravo." He picked up one menu from the two-inch stack. "How about steak? Which one of these is the best?"

Gretchen leaned over the island and shuffled through the paper, pulling out one that had a gold star drawn on the corner. "This one, definitely. Are you a rare or medium rare man?"

Daniel lifted his brows. "That's highly personal. Do you think you should ask me a question like that?"

Gretchen's tongue clicked against the roof of her mouth. "Oh, Daniel. Before you know it, you'll be answering in only one way. You'll be saying 'yes, darling' to everything."

Daniel took a quick drink from his beer. "If that's the case, I'm a medium rare man, darling." He lifted his bottle, toasted her, and added a devastatingly searing look.

Gretchen's skin was on fire. And then her ankle flipped, she lost her balance, but held onto the counter to mask the slip. Damn this man and his charm! *If I could only bottle it, women all over the world would be purchasing the product by the case.*

Chapter Eight

The next morning, Gretchen drank her tepid coffee and checked her day's schedule. She was still thinking about the lovely evening of steak at home with Daniel, until he announced that he needed to go.

"He is infuriating. He's a challenge, and he must be conquered. I will not surrender. And he has me blathering out loud." She looked over her to-do list which included visiting the Plaza store, checking on the caterer and musicians, and dropping off an additional liability contract to the aerial artists. But first, she began to formulate a plan. She decided if she was to gain Daniel's heart and his assorted other body parts, she must help him. She needed to investigate the deaths of those young men, especially that of the latest victim who meant so much to him.

She grabbed her phone and checked her contact list. She needed a reporter even if he was of the weasel variety. "Putnam? It's Gretchen Malloy. I need information, and you're the man to give it to me. There were two murders in an alley behind Laurent's. The police are considering it drug related. For all I know, they may not be investigating either one of the cases, but I intend to solve this mystery. This is very important–"

"Can I get a word in here?" the crusty reporter interrupted. Gretchen was usually annoying, mildly at the very least, but on a Monday morning she was overwhelmingly obnoxious. He needed more coffee and maybe a shot of something extra in it to deal with this woman. Leaning over and opening the bottom drawer of his desk, he pulled out a small bottle of whiskey and poured. "Look, Gretchen, I report about politicians, social status seekers, and power magnets. I'm sure you've been reading my weekly columns or watching me on the evening news at six. I'm all over social media, but I'm not on the police beat."

"I'm not calling about your social presence. I need help. Give me the contacts for the reporters who do follow crime in this city."

"And why on earth would I do this?"

Gretchen stuck out her tongue at the phone as she placed it on speaker mode. "You owe me after I've caught you snooping so many times where your bulbous nose shouldn't have been. Besides, I've given you great stories, including that feature on Marty and his senate race. I'll guarantee you an interview with him the night before the election."

Putnam didn't think twice, and it wasn't the whisky framing his decision. That story would be worth dealing with the stiletto menace. "Fine. I saw those stories about the boys. Who was the latest victim?"

Gretchen relayed what she gleaned from the very little Daniel was willing to share. "And Putnam, doesn't the mayor support the urban kids' leagues during the summer? Or is it year-round?"

Putnam shut his eyes to think. Gretchen had stopped talking, but he heard a cough. Then he heard a sigh. He needed to answer before she berated him for not answering quickly enough. "It's year-round now. He's very dedicated to those programs."

"I'll call Hal next. Keep me in the loop, Putnam. If you could be quick about it, that would be preferable."

On the other end of the line, the aging reporter mimicked Gretchen. "Fine. I'll get on it, but only because of the interview you promised." Click.

"Well, how rude," Gretchen yelled. "You are a squirrelly little man, but I need you right now."

She hit another button and left a message for the mayor. "Dear Hal, it's Gretchen. I need your assistance. Call me as soon as you can. It's a matter of life and death. Ta."

Hal immediately returned her call. "What's wrong? Have you been arrested again?"

"Mr. Mayor, I'm wonderful, but I need your invaluable help."

"Thank the heavens. I thought you had yourself embroiled in another murder."

"Actually, it's two murders this time."

Hal hit his forehead with his hand. "Geez, Gretchen. Can't you call that nice detective?"

"No, because I'm trying to help him, but he seemingly doesn't want my help. In fact, there are times I don't think he wants me, but then he does, and he kisses—"

"Stop," Hal interrupted quickly before Gretchen went into more detail. "I can't understand you when you ramble. Just tell me what is going on."

Gretchen stamped her foot. *Why are men so slow?* "There were two bodies found behind Laurent's. Both young men have participated in your urban sports programs. I know the latest victim, RJ, was a very good kid. There's no way he was involved in drugs, at least that's what a very reliable source told me. What is going on with your kids?"

Hal dropped back into his office chair. He had known Gretchen Malloy for so many years. Yes, the woman could be irrational and an obnoxious irritant. But just like with a clam, a little irritation usually resulted in a pearl. She had become a friend, one he could count on no matter what. She always was the first hand up to volunteer for his initiatives in the city. In politics, you seldom find a human like that.

"Gretchen, what's this about? I want the truth, woman."

Gretchen bit her bottom lip. She wondered how much knowledge he needed. But this was Hal. "My detective believes something bigger is going on. He also thinks these two young men should still be walking the streets of Kansas City. He seems torn up by their deaths, and…"

As Gretchen paused, Hal waited patiently. The great Malloy was being felled by a mere detective. "…I don't like seeing him this way. We've just begun, well, I don't know what we are beginning, but I want a chance with him. If he keeps worrying and working these murders, he won't have time for me."

Laughter emitted from the other side of the phone. "Do you know how shallow that just sounded?"

"It did, didn't it? I don't even really think that. I'm just worried about him. He seems to be a good man, and you and I both know how hard it is to find one in this city."

Hal understood better than most. He could count on one hand, the men he truly trusted. "Indeed I do. You've been a great friend to my family. Heck, you were the first one to suggest I run for mayor. What's your plan? I know you have one?"

"I just contacted that weasel Lawrence Putnam. He is useful for details and gossip. I'm planning a strategy, but I may need you. Are you in?"

Hal didn't hesitate. "I care about those kids, Gretchen. Of course, I am. At the very least I can offer the brawn."

"And that magic mayor key that gets you through every door in this city," Gretchen suggested coyly.

"Woman, what am I going to do with you?"

That was an easily answered question. "Just love me, and be my friend." Now, if she could just get another man to forget the friend word and to embrace the lover word, even if it was only physically, she'd be a much better woman. Her water bill would be lower too.

Chapter Nine

After Gretchen began to plan her attack to solve two murders, her confidence returned. "Detective, I'm going to help you whether you want me or not." She grimaced at the nagging thought that he might not desire her. *Perhaps my better days are behind me?*

The ups and downs of Gretchen's confidence were more up than down by the time she was walking from the parking garage to the department store on a perfect fall day. Gretchen was met by two whistles from hard hatted men four-stories high. They were hanging the banner for the re-opening.

Shielding her eyes with her hand, she looked up. "Hello, boys!" Gretchen added a little extra wiggle to her walk. The men clapped in appreciation. *Schmucks. Don't they know by now that real men don't treat real women like that? In their dreams would that behavior turn me on, or make me trot to them like a trained puppy.*

As she entered Laurent's, she was met by Elana, the franchise's liaison for the charity event. Elana was originally from San Antonio. Her hard hat barely fit over her full head of black hair that hung almost to her waist.

"Gretchen, I have a pink safety hat for you." She offered the headgear and a smile. "I'll walk you through the store, and we can confirm the set-up areas for the ice sculpture, the quartet, the jazz band, catering stations, and the rest of the entertainment. There will be a staging area for all of them in the customer service area."

Gretchen sought out one of the mirrors already placed on the newly stocked makeup counters. Placing her bag and folder next to it, she positioned her hard hat just right. "Is there any way I can keep this little number?"

Elana seemed confused. "Why on earth would you want it?"

Gretchen posed as she turned around. "To play construction, of course! I love to order around a man who is dressed in a toolbelt."

Elana's hand flew up to her mouth. "Oh my. He'll need dirty jeans, a tight shirt, and steel toe boots!"

Gretchen smacked her lips. "Oh no, he won't. The toolbelt will be sufficient."

Elana grabbed her arm playfully as though she were her new favorite sorority sister. "You are a naughty one. Let's get this walk through completed and grab a martini, unless you think it's too early?"

"It's never too early." Gretchen and Elana toured arm-in-arm. Minutes later they were examining the back of the store.

"Elana, is this the door to the alley?" Gretchen neared a large steel door.

"Yes. We're not using it right now. There have been two unfortunate deaths in the alley. Drugs are just killers. Why do they do this to themselves?"

Gretchen looked down. *Daniel doesn't believe that!* "May I–"

Elana's phone rang. She held up her hand and mouthed that she needed to take the call. She walked away leaving the event planner alone. Gretchen looked over the door. There didn't seem to be any alarms connected. Before she pressed on the door, it magically opened. She was shocked to see her busybody reporter on the other side.

"Ah, you're here."

"What are you doing here?" Gretchen balanced her file and purse on one of the storage room boxes. "Do you have news for me already?"

"I hate to admit it, Gretchen, but you're right about the death of those boys. Something stinks," Putnam commented harshly. "One of our neighborhood crime reporters is the lead on those stories, and she's just as curious as you. The police are tight-lipped, and they keep saying it has something to do with drugs. Both kids were clean, squeaky clean. RJ was an honor student, and he participated in several community service programs that the police sponsored. Our reporter thinks the first kid was actually working **with** the police! I'm not passing on this story, Gretchen. I'm in."

Gretchen inwardly sighed with relief. "Show me where all of this happened."

The reporter directed her out to the alley and placed a garbage can to hold the door open. Gretchen noticed trash and building materials on either side of the sliver of a delivery path. "I was here the other day, but I wasn't able to get back this far." She kicked a piece of loose asphalt that covered a small piece of paper. "I've got something here. There's a phone number."

Putnam accepted the item. "It's a local number. I'll check it out." He looked up to see the planner leaning down to view another item among the food wrappers and occasional soda can. "What is it now? The police went over every inch of this alley."

"I understand, but sometimes everyone can miss something. They wouldn't be looking for a nail with Fruity-Tutti polish." She held up her discovery. The shade appeared to be similar to one she used to wear.

The reporter snorted. "You've got to be kidding? Is that really a name?"

Gretchen stood up and kicked at the side of another discarded wrapper. "Yes, and I think I used to wear it. I kept seeing it on all my brides, but even I know when to give up on a fad. I now wear ruby red. You do know red is my signature color?"

Putnam gazed at the sky. "Lord, everyone in this bloody city knows that, woman. You wear animal prints, and you always wear those killer heels." He pointed at her stilettos.

"Must you be a bore?"

Putnam snarled. "Must **you** be **you**?"

Gretchen spotted another small item. "Yes, I must, and I'm damn good at being me." She crouched down and picked up an old St. Christopher's medal. Turning it over, she saw the monogram with the letters of **DWR**.

The reporter attempted to look over her shoulder, but the darn woman was taller than him in those heels. "What did you find now?"

Gretchen thought before answering. "It's just a medal." Her voice lowered so that the reporter barely heard her. *DWR, could this be Daniel's? If the monogram was correct and the surname is the middle initial, it would be for Daniel, Williams, and R what? Had he given it to one of the young men? And why do I even think this could've been his? Just intuition?* She pocketed it in her jacket.

"You know, we had that wind the other day. I bet this stuff was unearthed, and the police didn't even see it." Putnam pointed to an area by a stack of flattened cardboard boxes. "I guess this is where one of the kids bit the dust."

Gretchen walked to his side. "I told you that sometimes even the police aren't looking for the right things. Is that blood?" Her hand shook as she directed his attention to the rusty stains on the concrete wall.

"Maybe. I don't know stuff like that. You're the one who walked over a dead body."

"I didn't mean to do it. Sometimes, I'm just the lucky one who is embroiled in the happenings of our fair city."

The reporter kicked at a few pieces of trash to hopefully find his own evidence. "Well, I think you have two murders on your hands, Malloy. You may have to add private investigator to your business card. In the meantime, I'll keep digging. I'll find out why the police didn't find this stuff. That could be important, right?"

Gretchen's finger rubbed the medal in her pocket. There was a story here, but whose was the question. "Sometimes, Putnam, it is just the wind that moves things around. And sometimes, the ordinary is unseen." *Add private investigator? What an amazing idea. The print could be in blood red.*

Putnam nodded. "Gretchen, I'll deny I said this, but it takes a special person to care about something like this. If it weren't for you, those poor kids might be overlooked."

"No one deserves to be overlooked or marginalized," Gretchen said softly. She patted the reporter's arm. "I really do appreciate anything you could do."

"You're worried about something, aren't you?"

"No, I can handle anything." Gretchen flipped her hair off of one shoulder. "You should know that by now, you strange little man. I'm just concerned, and I'm thinking about all the work I have ahead of me."

The jaded reporter smiled. Their moment had passed. "Of course. You have that big event, and you don't want anything to go wrong, do you? It's always about you."

Gretchen smiled. "When one is as fabulous as me, I have a reputation to maintain."

"By the way, what all goes into planning a shindig like this? I usually just show up for the shrimp cocktail and the booze." Putnam pulled a cigar from the inside pocket of his jacket.

Gretchen shook her head in dismay. "You sorry little man. There is so much. Today, I've already confirmed delivery times for vendors. The department store liaison and

I are walking through so we know where everyone needs to set up. Logistics can be a nightmare if you're incompetent. Luckily, I'm not. I don't want any surprises."

"Like a bomb going off?"

Gretchen frowned. "That's not even funny. What is wrong with you? There's always so much to do. After I finish here, I'll drop legal documents for the aerial artist and her group."

Putnam spit out the end of his cigar. "What the heck is an aerial artist?"

"You know the term trapeze?"

"Like at the circus?" He lit up his cigar and began to puff, a light gray smoke circling his head like a target zone for the Airborne.

"Exactly. There are new terms for everything and everyone." Gretchen stepped away from the reporter to be upwind from his disgusting cheap cigars.

"Gretchen, old girl the world is changing, and frankly, we're getting too old to change."

His lament resonated in Gretchen's heart. "Truthfully, I agree with you, but I'm fighting it yearly."

Putnam nodded in agreement. "Those birthdays do sneak up on you, but I must admit you do battle them well."

Normally, Gretchen would thank the man, but considering who the compliment was coming from, she remained silent as she had when he admitted she was special. The journalist shrugged and turned. She watched

Putnam shaking his head as he walked away. Her smile faded quickly as she bit her lip. There was more wrong than the changing times or the weasel offering her a kind word or two. As she pulled the medal into the daylight, her concern intensified. *Something's very wrong, and I just know my detective is involved.*

As though he heard her think of him, the detective's name came up on her phone as it buzzed. "Detective," Gretchen purred. "This is a lovely surprise."

"Where are you right now?"

Gretchen looked up and down the alley. No one. She stepped back, almost falling backward into the cardboard so she could peek at the roofline. No one. She checked for security cameras. They hadn't been installed yet. *He can't possibly see me, can he?*

She decided to lie, but just a little. "I'm working down at the event site. What can I do for you?"

"Meet me for a late lunch in an hour?"

Finally, some interest. "Lovely. Where?"

"Finley's at Westport?"

Gretchen enjoyed that restaurant, and this would be the perfect day to lunch on the outside patio. "I'll see you there."

"Perfect. I have to go."

Perhaps we can have dessert back at my apartment? No, I have work to do and mysteries to solve!

Gretchen finished her meeting with Elana and nailed down security details that concerned her. They were anticipating the attendance of some of the richest patrons in the city, and the event was featuring millions in diamonds including very rare red ones. She couldn't wait to see those precious stones, or even touch one or two. But those little beauties weren't coming home with her. Rare meant expensive. Gretchen would rather upgrade her wardrobe or cruise around the world ten times.

As Gretchen headed out to deliver the aerialist's contract, she realized she'd only be blocks away from her afternoon interlude with Daniel. She walked slowly up the concrete stairs to the performer's Westport apartment building. Westport was one area of the city that had a true New York City bohemian vibe. Young people filled every inch of the area on a warm summer night. Artists of every variety sold their masterpieces to young couples setting up their first homes together. As she raised her hand to knock, a young lady in a large flowing shirt and leggings popped out.

"Are you Ms. Malloy?"

"Yes, and you are Larkin?"

The young woman nodded, smiling widely, and sticking out her hand for a quick shake. "I thought it was you. You look so metropolitan, and I love your heels. When I get old, I want to wear those kinds of expensive beauties."

Gretchen would've burned the little ninny with her x-ray vision, if she had that super-power. Gretchen's eyes narrowed into thin slits of mild rage. "This packet needs to be reviewed. We'll need signatures and your liability information returned before next week. The jugglers will need to sign these too since they'll be moving among the guests. You can drop all of this off to Elana at the store."

"I can get that done. Elana got us this gig. She and I met at Sweeney's bar last year, and she saw my group perform at the art gallery when they had *The Sky's The Limit* event last summer."

"Ah, that was you. I went to that." Gretchen remembered that evening. She'd accompanied a banker, and he was the biggest bore she had ever dated. After that night, there was not a second. "You are very good. Have you and Elana discussed your setup?"

"Yes. I'll be hanging from the ceiling and sitting in a red circular support just above the ice sculpture. At the height of our show, I'll reach down with a goblet and scoop into the ice, pulling out the fake diamonds. I'll pretend to drink the cup, but instead, I'll let the stones fall. At the same time, the champagne will begin to flow from the sculpture."

Gretchen admired the woman's enthusiasm and knowledge of the details. "The ice sculpture will be a large glass. It should be very dramatic with you up there."

"It'll be something." The young lady looked down at the brown manila envelope. "Thanks for dropping this off, Gretch."

Nails on a chalkboard or sneakers on a gym floor couldn't possibly be any worse sound than the misuse of her name. Gretchen looked at the time. *If I had ten minutes, I would tell her off, or cut off that cute little braided ponytail.* Instead, Gretchen put on her fake smile, turned on her expensive heels and quickly left to meet Daniel. After searching for a parking space, she began running toward the restaurant. She slowed as she noticed him sitting at a courtyard table.

As she came closer to him, he stood. He offered a quick kiss on her cheek and moved the chair out. "You look like you've had a busy day."

Her loss of breath wasn't just from hurrying as she looked up into his eyes from her seated position. "I just came from one of the performers for the event. I could've eviscerated her."

Daniel laughed as he sat across from her. "You probably shouldn't tell a cop that."

"It was warranted. She called me Gretch."

"Then we must flog her," Daniel said sternly. "That's inexcusable."

Without thinking, Gretchen reached over and grasped his hand. "See, you do understand."

Daniel nodded as he looked down at her hand. "I try. I really do try." A shared moment of silence was followed by menu gazing.

Thankfully, the print was large enough that Gretchen didn't require her readers. "What looks good to you?"

Daniel Williams leaned back to study her. She had an energy that commanded attention. He noticed two women at the next table who were obviously discussing Gretchen's fashion choices. She was flawless, yet professional. He moved closer to her until his lips were almost touching the menu. *Why does she always put me in a position where I have two choices to answer her? I'll just say it.*

"You do."

Gretchen dropped the paper onto the table. "Do I? That's very kind of you." It wasn't as though she hadn't had her pants charmed off of her before in her lifetime. Powerful men elicited passion. This wasn't one of those times. Daniel was just a detective. He didn't have power or the purse, but he certainly had the charm. She imagined he also had the stamina to make her want to stay in bed for days. "Let's order. I'm famished."

"Gretchen, did you hear me?"

The server suddenly hovered over them. Gretchen ordered as did her companion. She waited until their drinks were delivered before she addressed the charmer.

"Daniel, I did hear you. That is so kind of you because I'm sure I look a bit frazzled." *I want to ask you about the medal, dear man.*

"I was attempting to be romantic. I know we haven't known each other that long, and I wanted you to know that I'm interested. I was thinking about you today. I realize I haven't been that responsive. The truth is I've had a hard time with intimacy."

Gretchen's concern was overwhelming. "Oh, my. Is that what the problem is? Are you being treated by a doctor?"

Daniel, amused and stunned, laughed nervously. "No, I'm fine in that department. I meant lowering my shield and getting to know you."

"Ah, so you're not talking about knowing me in a biblical connotation?"

This time, Daniel laughed out loud. "You are a very sexual person."

Gretchen's smile thinned. "Yes. Is there something wrong with that? I like being a woman. You're a man I like. This all should be so easy."

The detective rimmed his glass with his finger, avoiding her eyes at all cost. "I'm different. It seems nothing comes easy for me. It should." His voice was so low it was barely audible. "I've had a very good life. I–"

Does my Daniel have a secret, or more than one?

"Honestly, I've never met anyone like you, Gretchen. I thoroughly enjoy your company for some bizarre reason."

Gretchen's eyes widened. "Excuse me?"

Daniel leaned back in his chair to place distance between them. "Oh come on. We met over a dead body. You gave me headaches for weeks. We are so different. But, I laugh when I'm with you. I relish every second. I enjoy the food more, and the wine and beer always tastes better when you pour them in my glass. I needed to see you today. Have I redeemed myself?"

Gretchen squinted. She took her time reaching in her purse for her sunglasses. "I suppose. Those were lovely words, but I've been charmed before. Prior to you, other men have enjoyed what I have served them."

Daniel chuckled. He reached for her hand and captured it in his. "There you go again. Are we speaking about the food and drink or–"

"You are nothing but perceptive, Daniel. That's why I like being with you. I'm curious though. Haven't you ever been around someone like me?"

Daniel Williams paused. *How much should I tell her? How much can I tell her? I've always hidden my life.* "I've met many women like you, but they weren't as full of life as you are. They had expensive clothing and designer shoes, although you have them beat with the height of your heels. I'm used to being around women like you, but there is no one like you."

Sunglasses could conceal so much, and Gretchen was using that aspect of her accessory to the max. "And there never will be, Daniel."

As they ate their lunch, there was a little small talk before Gretchen's fork was raised in the air toward her companion.

"Daniel, I've noticed you love to verbally spar with me. Did you do that with other women you've known?"

Daniel gulped. "Um, yes, with one."

"Your ex-wife?"

This was going to go terribly wrong either way…if he told the truth or if he lied. It would be better to just rip the band aid off of this one. "No, my mother."

"I remind you of your mother?"

"I never said that," Daniel answered loudly to match her tone. A man at another table looked up from his phone. The detective smiled to calm his demeanor. "I'm saying I used to enjoy a good conversation with her like I do with you. She's a very formidable and intelligent woman too."

Gretchen finished chewing a piece of lettuce. "I was wondering because I certainly hope you never kiss your mother the way you kiss me."

Daniel gritted his teeth. "Ah, it's those kisses. Our verbal sparring is usually flirtatious, sexually charged. You need to know I don't move as fast as you do. I take my time, and believe me when it finally happens, I'll knock your heels off, okay?"

Gretchen lowered her sunglasses. She gulped and remained silent.

"Call me old-fashioned, Gretchen. You can make fun of me. You can fall in and out of bed for enjoyment. I can't. I grew out of that stage in my life."

Gretchen placed her fork down. "I do enjoy a morning, afternoon, or evening tumble. I am a grown woman with no regrets, mister. Apparently, you have some puritanical baggage in your closet."

Daniel threw his napkin and lifted his hand to signal for the check. "I don't have a puritanical bone in my body, but I like to be careful and prudent."

Gretchen threw her own napkin as though they were football umpires finding multiple infractions in a tight game. "Who uses the word prudent?"

"I do." As the server came to his side, Williams offered his credit card. He smiled at the young lady as she hurried away.

Gretchen crossed her arms in front of her. "Really? I don't get jealous."

"Why should you? There's nothing between us except for good conversation and the occasional kiss."

Gretchen reached for her bag and began searching for her car keys. "That's exactly correct, detective. We've had some good times together, albeit platonic."

The server returned his card. He thanked her and handed back the signed receipt. Daniel stood up quickly. "Shall we go?"

"I think we should. Obviously, lunch is over. Thank you for the meal." She walked in front of him through the courtyard. She felt his hand at the lowest part of her back until they arrived at the sidewalk.

"I'm parked this way."

Gretchen pointed in the opposite direction. "And I'm this way."

Daniel hid his eyes as donned his sunglasses. "Gretchen, I need an invitation to your event."

Gretchen balanced heavier on her left foot, posing as bored as she possibly could. "And a plus one for you?"

Williams hung his head. "I was hoping I could go with you, but–"

"Fine. I'll take you, but you'll do whatever I tell you. You'll be on my turf, detective, and you won't be in charge. I am. Got it?"

"You're in charge. Fine."

Gretchen waved her finger in his face. "Gretchen Malloy is an exclusive product, buddy. They call me the 'day of witch', only they usually replace the w with a b. I am an expert at planning the perfect event, and so it must be. My trust level with you is very low. I think you have a secret, and it has something to do with your young friends. It's commendable, the generosity of your time with those kids. Just when I think you're the best man I've met in a long time, you tell me I remind me of your mother."

Daniel placed a hand on each of her shoulders. "That's a lot to take in, but yes this all has to do with the murders, and no you don't remind me of my mother. Maybe you could just introduce me as your date for the evening?"

"Or my assistant? No one ever asks who the assistant is. Yes, we will work with that. I need to go. Could you please release me?"

"Not yet, but I'll let you go back to work after this."

Gretchen realized what was about to happen on the Westport sidewalk, on a perfect fall day, in front of couples dining and joggers passing by. His attack was soft. He brushed her lips with his. His arms moved to embrace her softly but firmly in his grasp. He kissed her quickly, then lingered on the side of cheek. He held her tighter and closer than he ever had before. This man was getting under her skin in a way she'd never felt before. When he finally drew back, her ankle gave way, sending her off balance. Again.

Daniel caught her before she fell. "Are you okay?"

"I wasn't expecting that. I'll be prepared if there's a next time."

Daniel's laughter rumbled from deep in his chest. "Oh, there'll be a next time. It's too much fun keeping you off balance." He pointed at her heels. "You might consider wearing sneakers or flats when you're with me from now on. See you later, boss. Tootles."

He saluted her with two fingers and walked away leaving her completely out of sorts. Gretchen stomped her feet and screamed out, "You can't use my signature word. The next thing you know you'll be wearing red!"

As Gretchen drove back to her apartment, she touched her lips. They still felt as though they were on fire. *There's something holding him back, and it's not the bloody age difference! Maybe he thinks I'm in love with Chance? No, it's because he thinks I'm loose, and I think he is stodgy. Maybe Daniel grew up in an Amish community? What is his connection to the boys? What is his middle name? One thing is for sure. There's more to all of this than I'm seeing. I need to use my special skills and get to the bottom of this before I capture Daniel in a small space and ravish him. Or vice-a-versa if I can coax him into sin.*

"What a delightful idea!"

Chapter Ten

"Gretchen, you aren't going to believe whose number that is. Do you remember the detective who tried to nail you for the Hampton boy's murder?"

"Putnam, if you don't spit it out, I'll reach through this phone and twist you into a weasel pretzel."

Putnam huffed. "Fine. I was building suspense. The number belongs to that detective." He began to laugh.

"It can't be," Gretchen murmured. Quickly, she scanned her contacts on her cell. It wasn't Daniel's number. "Putnam, is it his work number?"

"Yes, direct to his desk. I'm thinking about visiting the good old detective today. Do you want to go along and watch him squirm?"

"No," Gretchen said forcefully. "Just wait. Let's gather more information before you do that." *Let's never do that at least until I figure out if he's involved in these murders. No, he can't be.*

"Sometimes I don't understand you," Putnam answered. "I'll wait, and I'll keep looking."

"And I'll do the same," Gretchen lied. "Lawrence, thank you for helping me."

The journalist was surprised at Gretchen's tone of despondency, and the fact she called him by his first name. "Whatever this is all about, I'll help you in any way I can."

"That is very kind of you, Lawrence."

As the call completed, Putnam shook his head. Something was very wrong. He looked at his notepad and wrote another item onto his list. Yes, he needed to call the mayor and tell him that Gretchen Malloy was in trouble.

Daniel called three times that day, and Gretchen allowed every call to go to voicemail. She didn't know what to say to him. She was caught up on every bit of work for the next month. It was late afternoon when she stood on her balcony and looked toward the Plaza. She was tired of feeling useless. It was past time to be proactive. Heading to her closet, she retrieved a dark washed pair of jeans, a black turtleneck, and her leather jacket. She slipped on a pair of shiny boots, and searched through the shelves until found a black knit hat.

After a light dinner, she walked a few blocks to an outside coffee stand. She found a table and waited until the sky was pitch black. It was time to make her move.

Gretchen entered the alley slowly. She turned on her small flashlight and began to search again. Noticing that the security cameras were still not installed, she made a mental note to contact Elana tomorrow. She scanned the low wall that connected with the parking garage.

Her light floated just above the fence line. Something shined. She moved the light over the area once more and saw the same reflection. Gretchen looked around to find something to stand on. As she began to shove a small wood box over, she felt a hand on her shoulder. Gretchen swept around, flailing her flashlight against her attacker.

"Gretchen, it's me."

Her weapon had struck the very large chest of the mayor. "Hal? What the devil are you doing here?"

"I could ask you the same thing. And you hurt me. I'm just happy you didn't hit me with a rock or we'd be looking for another mayor."

Gretchen shined her light into Hal's face as though she was an interrogator in an old detective movie. "Why are you here?"

"Putnam was worried you might do something crazy. He was concerned about you, and so am I."

"Where is the little weasel?"

Putnam appeared from around the corner. He held a bag of popcorn in his hand. "I was parking the car down the block. What have you found now, super sleuth?"

Gretchen mulled the term over in her brain. *I like it.* "Wait, where's your security detail, Hal?"

Putnam snickered as Hal shrugged. "You should've seen it, Gretchen. The duly elected mayor of our fair city crawled out his bathroom window at the back of the house and ran like he was in his golden days of NFL to my waiting car. I didn't know he was still that fast, or that he could collapse his body into such a small space."

Gretchen shook her head. "You two are crazy."

Hal pointed his finger at his friend. "And you're crazy to come back here. What have you found this time?"

"There's something up there on the fence, but I can't reach it."

"You could if I hoisted you up," Hal suggested. He knew he could throw Putnam at least fifteen feet and never break a sweat.

Putnam crunched on a kernel. "I'll watch. I should've brought a lawn chair."

The journalist didn't see Gretchen's scathing glare in the dark. "That's what you do best, you weasel."

"Your arrows will not pierce me," he answered blandly.

"I can think of a part of your body I'd like to pierce," Gretchen muttered.

Hal snickered. "Come on. Let's get you up there, and then we can all go home and leave this to the police. I don't need this splashed over every news station."

Gretchen stood beneath the area and readied herself. The mayor looked down at her shoes. "Oh, hell no. Take those killers off. I'm not putting you on my shoulders while you're wearing those heels."

Gretchen agreed and removed her boots immediately. She stood on the box she had found as Hal leaned over. In one move, she was about ten feet in the air and within inches of the item. Her hand reached around until she caught something in her grasp. It was a key.

"I've got it!" Gretchen announced.

"Um, guys, we have a small problem." Putnam stopped munching.

"The small problem is you," Gretchen added. "Hal, get me down."

"This is going to be harder than picking you up." The mayor uneasily began the few steps back to the wood box that had acted as their platform. "Gretchen, stop moving around up there."

"Your neck is bony," she complained. She planted both hands on Hal's head for balance. "Don't you dare drop me."

Putnam didn't know what to be more concerned about. "Guys."

Hal turned slowly around as Gretchen and he yelled, "What?"

The mayor held tightly to Gretchen's legs as they both saw Putnam standing next to…

"Detective?" Hal asked.

Daniel Williams leaned against the wall of the building. His face was void of emotion. Gretchen knew that look. He had it on his face the first time she'd met him. *It's somewhere in between constipation and exasperation.*

"Hello Daniel," Gretchen added nervously.

"I expect this behavior out of you," he said quietly as he pointed at the balancing woman. "I could even expect it out of a journalist, but the mayor? By the way, your security detail is looking for you. They were concerned when they saw a man running from your home and getting into Mr. Putnam's car."

Hal smiled. "Let's get you down, Gretchen." Slowly, he leaned over and removed his precious cargo from his shoulders one leg at a time. It wasn't pretty, but Gretchen was down safely. He rubbed his hands as though he was finished with a project. "I guess I better get going. Putnam, you want to drop me off?"

Williams pointed around the corner. "Your detail is waiting for you, sir. Have a good night."

"I'll be going too. Nice seeing you, detective." Putnam shuffled off into the darkness. Hal followed leaving Gretchen and the detective standing in a dark alley. Gretchen's eyes were averted. Daniel's eyes were on fire.

"What in the hell were you thinking? I knew you'd do something like this. By the way, this outfit is nicer than your dumpster duds. Get your boots on. I'm taking you home."

His stern direction didn't set well. "I can take myself back home, thank you."

Daniel pointed at her heels. "Put the damn boots on."

It was easier just to do what he ordered, but she never took too fondly to a man telling her–not asking her–what to do. She slowly zipped them. The key she had discovered was secure in the secret inside pocket of her jacket. She stood and began to walk away, but the detective had other ideas.

"You stop," he commanded as he touched her arm. "Don't make me pick you up and throw you in my car."

Gretchen shook her hair as she removed her hat. "Oh, now you want to get romantic!"

Daniel grabbed her gently. He pulled her tightly against his chest. "I know you want to help, but trust me when I say this is bigger than what you're seeing. Please, for the love of God, trust me."

She could see his eyes shine in the darkness. *He is a good man, isn't he?* She caressed his cheek. "Let me help you."

"Did you find anything?"

"No."

"That's the least you have ever said. You're lying." Daniel smiled. He was beginning to read her. *What had Agent Pierce said? His wife could read his 'tells'?* "Give me what you found."

"I don't have anything."

Daniel held her a little tighter. "Do I need to search you?"

Gretchen placed one finger up to her lips. "That's an interesting question. It could be very enjoyable."

Daniel released her and stepped back. "Fine. You're going to do what you want. I can't stop you, but please be careful. And if you know something, you do need to tell me. Now, let's get you home."

Gretchen opened her mouth to respond, but she quickly stopped. They walked together to his car, and Daniel drove her home. He reached over and caught her hand before she exited.

"I do care about you."

Gretchen slipped her hand under her jacket and removed the key. "I found this. For your information, the store's liaison Elana has a similar one. It looks like the key she used when she was retrieving the store's corporate credit card from the safe. I noticed the red line on it. See?"

"I see. Thank you," Daniel murmured. "Did you find anything else tonight?"

Gretchen garnered every bit of her ability to act. "No, we didn't find anything else tonight." *I am telling the truth about tonight.*

Gretchen gave him a peck on the cheek and retreated to his vehicle, never looking back. Daniel had his secrets. She did too. She had a rather large one now…she had never lied to a man she loved.

Chapter Eleven

With Putnam's help, Gretchen set up a meeting with RJ's mother. As she parked in front of the small home, she noticed it was the only property that featured a white picket fence and an impeccably mowed lawn. Wind chimes and potted mum plants greeted her as she stepped onto the open porch. On any other workday, Gretchen wouldn't be caught in a pair of jeans, but today she wore pressed jeans with a pair of ballet flats, a silk blouse, and a dark navy double breasted suit jacket. This was as relaxed as she ever allowed herself to dress in public, but she was attempting to dress like a reporter. Well, it was her version of a reporter. She still sported her gold bracelets, hoop earrings, and designer watch.

Gretchen was greeted by a petite woman dressed in jeans and a sweater. "Mrs. Fremont, I'm Gretchen Malloy. Thank you for meeting with me."

She opened the door quickly and invited her in. "I just appreciate Mr. Putnam and you looking into my son's murder." She offered her visitor a seat on the couch. She began to pour a cup of coffee. "Do you take it black?"

"Yes, ma'am." Gretchen cringed as the evil word flew from her own mouth.

"Please have a piece of cake. It's my mother's recipe. She used to be a cook at one of the hotels. How can I help you?"

"Actually, I wanted to know more about RJ. How long had he been working at the grocery store?"

Mrs. Cilia Fremont smiled. "His first day working there was on his sixteenth birthday. Most kids would grumble about that, but he was so proud. Of course, he didn't want to disappoint the detective who helped him get the job."

Gretchen's left brow raised. "That's Detective Daniel Williams, correct?"

"Oh, yes. Detective Williams helped both of my boys. My oldest, Micah, is back east at an Ivy League school. The detective set him up there. In my wildest dreams I never would've imagined my son thriving at a place like that."

Gretchen mustered up every bit of thespian skill in her to not act shocked. "When did the boys meet the detective?"

"I think he had just come to Kansas City. He became involved in the police's afterhours program. The next thing I knew he was bringing Micah home one afternoon. My son had shoplifted. Thankfully, the sports store dropped the charges, but the detective made him work it off at that store. Micah began to take pride in himself. His grades soared, and he began talking about the future."

The aroma from the cake began to entice Gretchen. She couldn't deny it anymore. Reaching over toward the knife, she smiled. "May I? It smells heavenly."

"Please. It has caramel and pecans with a little apple in it. I hope you don't have a nut allergy."

"Oh no." Gretchen took a bite and marveled at the moistness. "I need an allergy to all food. I have to work out like a fool to just keep my size, but as I get older it becomes harder and harder to succeed."

Mrs. Fremont surveyed her visitor. "Oh, honey, you don't need to worry about your weight. You are stacked in all the right places."

Had Gretchen been thirty years younger she would've been blushing. "Mrs. Fremont, what do you think happened to RJ? Have you heard anything?"

Tears glistened in the mother's eyes. "I've heard nothing. The police want me to believe my boy was into drugs. He wasn't. I think gang members came into the store, and RJ said something or maybe even heard something."

"Do you think he became involved in something he couldn't control?"

Mrs. Fremont tilted her head. "Control? Yes. There was something. Eat your cake, and I'll get his diary." She soon returned with a small journal. She turned the pages slowly as she wiped away a few more tears. "Here it is. It's about a security company called Control Systems."

As Mrs. Fremont passed the book to Gretchen, she pulled her glasses out of her bag and devoured the pages. "Has the detective seen this?"

"No, I haven't shown anyone. You just made me remember that name. RJ heard that something was going down, but he said it was supposed to be this summer."

My event was supposed to be the Fourth of July weekend, but the construction was delayed. Gretchen handed the intimate writing back to RJ's mother. "Mrs. Fremont, you need to show this to the detective. It's very important." She looked down at her watch. "I should really go. I thank you for your time, and for that delicious cake."

Gretchen caught a peek of the family photos on the hall's wall. It was heartbreaking to see a lovely family now broken. A large portrait featured the young boys, Mrs. Fremont, and another gentleman. "You have a beautiful family."

"It was. My husband passed away from cancer ten years ago, and now RJ is gone. Do you have children?"

Gretchen gulped. She never regretted not having a family until someone asked her that question. She hated the pity evoked when she answered negatively. "No, I was never blessed with children or a husband. You were very lucky."

"Luck had nothing to do with it. It was a lot of hard work," the widow admitted. She smiled as she patted the supposed news reporter. "Children and a husband aren't necessary for a good life. We make our own lives with God's grace."

Gretchen nodded and pretended to nonchalantly peruse the other photos. She stopped in front of the last one. "This is RJ, right?"

Mrs. Fremont smiled. "Oh yes."

"That's a St. Christopher's medal."

"You have a good eye. The detective gave that to RJ this past Christmas. My son had made the honor roll that semester, and he was beginning to apply to colleges. That medal was the detective's. He said it protected him when he was in the Navy. He flew missions over Afghanistan. He's a hero."

Gretchen only nodded and headed to the door. She was stopped by a hand on her shoulder. "Ms. Malloy, I just remembered. I didn't get that medal back with RJ's personal items. I hope it isn't lost. I'd like to return it to the detective, to protect him again."

Without thinking, Gretchen hugged Cilia Fremont. "I meet a lot of people and most of them are shallow and self-absorbed. On any given day, people might describe me in the same way, but I'm blessed. I have met you, and I'll do what I can to get you the answers you deserve. I'll also find that medal and get it back to that hero detective."

Mrs. Fremont nodded. "Thank you, ma'am."

And for that one moment, Gretchen appreciated the usually cringe worthy term only because a great woman had said it.

Chapter Twelve

Gretchen buzzed Daniel up later that evening. She stood in her open doorway once more, holding his favorite beer in one hand and her glass of wine in the other.

"Daniel, this is a nice surprise," she purred as he grabbed the brew quickly and strode deliberately inside the apartment. He plopped on the couch.

"You like surprises, don't you? I thought you learned your lesson the other night, but today…what were you thinking?"

Gretchen closed her door and leaned against it as she watched his anger building. He knows.

"I thought you could use a little more help. I found that key the other night."

Daniel downed a gulp of beer. "You teamed up with Putnam the ferret and pretended you were a reporter? You bothered that poor woman?"

Gretchen remained silent as she sat down across from him. *Their relationship wouldn't be going anywhere if he thought he could have unjustified indignation. It wasn't attractive.* "You are right. Putnam is a ferret. You are wrong. I didn't bother her. In fact, I think she needed to talk. I'm trying to help you. I thought–"

"No, you didn't," Daniel interrupted. "You never think. You jump in headfirst. It almost landed you in jail with that murdered groom escapade. You didn't stop until you were at the wrong end of a gun. This time, you've put the mayor's life in danger, and you involved a news reporter who doesn't even cover crime. I saw him on television covering politics. I'm not allowed to cover Tito's investigation, and my colleagues are only focusing on this being a drug case. I barely get to work on RJ's death.

Gretchen placed her wine glass on the table in front of her and leaned in. "But you are working on it."

"Of course I am."

Gretchen admired how he could look like he always belonged in her home. He finished the bottle of beer and stretched his arms across the back of the couch.

"If you could lower your voice, we could discuss this like two civilized people."

Daniel stretched his neck, moving it from side to side. "Fine. What? One of these times you're going to get yourself into trouble, and I won't be there to rescue you."

Gretchen moved to tower over him. "Look, mister, I don't need rescuing. I'm just trying to help."

"Why? What is it to you?"

"God help me, but I apparently care about you, and you are hurting over Tito's death, and especially RJ's." *Really, God help me, please.*

She sat down slowly by his side as though he was a wounded animal who could turn on her at any moment. He lowered his arms and hid his head in his hands. "Fine. What have you learned?"

I like him defeated. He's more pliable. "I have tons of information. You can look over my notes. Every piece of evidence I have ties to my event. I don't know why, how, or what yet. It's almost like the time I had this wedding at the art museum. I just knew some idiot groomsman was going to ruin a million-dollar painting, and it happened within five minutes."

Daniel looked up in wonderment. "Do I want to know what he did?"

Gretchen wrinkled her nose as though she had smelled a fowl fragrance. "You can imagine. No one could act fast enough when he unzipped his pants and–"

Daniel began to laugh uncontrollably. He held his hands up and gathered hers in his. "Stop. I can't stand some of these stories. I used to think you made them all up."

Gretchen sat up straight. "I do not. Most of the time real life is so much more than what you see in the movies."

They both looked down at their combined hands. "Gretchen, this is dangerous, and you're right. We believe something big is going to happen at your event."

Gretchen nudged his body with her own. "I suppose you'll have to be my date, and my assistant for the night."

He playfully feigned embarrassment. "Ms. Malloy, are you trying to seduce me?"

Gretchen removed her hand and shoved his arm hard. "I've been trying to do that for weeks now. I have my doubts that an invitation to an event is going to change anything except make me more frustrated when I see you in a tux. Oh, you'll have to rent one."

Daniel only nodded. He chose not to acknowledge anything she'd just said except for the fashion request. "I'll make sure I'm dressed and all cleaned up so I can escort the prettiest woman to the party."

"Escort, huh?" Gretchen smiled. "I'm starving. What are we ordering tonight?"

Daniel left her side to take his empty bottle to the kitchen. "Let me take you out."

"No. I've taken off some of my makeup. Besides, you can't afford to keep taking me out."

Her guest winked. "Don't worry about that. I like to treat you."

"And I was on the police board once." She stopped talking when she saw the shock on his face. "Yes, I was. I'm very influential, buddy. On the board I saw what our force makes, and you don't get paid enough. You can't afford my lifestyle."

Daniel leaned over. He kissed the top of her head. "Let me worry about what I can afford. Besides, aren't you the one who is always saying you can't judge anyone by their home, car, and even their clothes?"

"I hate it when men actually listen to me. It places me in a delicate position of having to agree with them." She pouted half-heartedly. "But really, I'd prefer to eat in tonight. Please." *I have to return something to you.*

Daniel's hands flew up in surrender. "Fine. How about curry? I know this little place."

Gretchen frowned. "Curry bothers my stomach. How about Thai?"

"That does sound good. I have a place on speed dial, and they deliver."

While Daniel ordered their dinners, Gretchen strolled to the kitchen to pull the plates and silverware. She watched him slip off his shoes as he walked around. He balanced the phone on his neck while rolling up his shirt sleeves and pulling at his tie. He threw it over one of her bar chairs. He seemed so very comfortable as he fingered the two top buttons of his shirt. He seemed to be home. Gretchen felt as though she were a star-struck fan. *How has this happened to me after all of these years? Lily says I've closed my heart. Well, apparently it's open for business now.*

Her adoration was fractured when she saw the text that had just popped up on her phone. Chance's daughter had just had a baby girl.

"The food will be here in about thirty minutes."

Gretchen shoved her phone into a pocket. "Thirty minutes? Wonderful. Why don't you tell me about your day."

Daniel sat at the kitchen island. "I'd rather hear what you and the reporter have learned so far. Do you have any other secrets?"

Gretchen flinched. The time had come, and it had come before dinner. Her stomach growled on cue. *Damn.* "I went to the alley prior to the other night, and I did find a couple of things."

Daniel didn't flinch. He touched his forehead. "I think I'm getting a headache. This better be the end of the evidence you've found."

"It is," Gretchen whispered. She turned to a side drawer and removed a baggie.

Daniel examined the nail. "What is this?"

"Acrylic and in the shade of Fruity-Tutti."

"What? How do you know that?"

Gretchen batted her eyelashes. "Come now, you should know by now I know all things fashion, including trends and fads. Besides, half of my brides were wearing this, and they still carry it at my spa. They go through so much of it with the young girls that they run out of their supply constantly. By the way, I visited them this morning, and they confirmed that I was correct. Oh, and the design on it comes from a nail salon down the street from that nice Westport restaurant where we met."

Daniel shook his head. *What am I going to do with her? Get more aspirin.* "You checked with your spa, and then you confirmed with the nail salon? Do they know who the customer was?"

"Dear Daniel," Gretchen groaned. "They can't tell you that."

"It's not like there's a client privilege when getting your nails done." He began to chuckle to lighten the pressure in his right temple.

Gretchen sighed. "It's not that. They can't tell you because several ladies use that design. It's very popular. One of the pop singers is wearing it on one nail. I think she designed a jewelry line based on that design. But, I have seen the color on someone lately."

"Who?"

"Our performer at the event. When I gave her the contracts, she had the color on her toes and hands."

Daniel's interest was mildly piqued. "But you said girls are into that."

"But they aren't into having a broken nail…just one broken nail that was missing."

"And you have all of this information in the file you gave me?"

Gretchen nodded. "And I have more notes from today." She patted the medal that was hidden in her pocket.

"What else did you find? I thought you said you found more than one item?"

Gretchen sighed. This could go very well, but it would probably go very badly. "Daniel, I know so little about you. What is your middle name?"

Daniel stood up quickly. "What? Why do you need to know that? Am I one of your suspects now?"

"Please sit down. I need to know."

He lowered slowly into the chair. He noticed her hand was patting a side pocket. "What do you have in there?" He pointed at her.

"What is your middle name?"

Daniel shifted nervously and attempted to avert her gaze. She lowered her head. "Fine. It's Revere."

Oh no. "Revere? Did your parents love American history, or were they into one if by land, two if by sea?" Gretchen snorted at her joke.

"Our family is from Boston. It's an old family name on my mother's side."

Gretchen marveled at the information. "Really? That is amazing. I'm assuming it is that Revere?"

"Yep, that Revere." Daniel watched as she slyly backed away, edging to one of the drawers. "And don't even think about hiding it. Hand it over. Now."

His tone was more like an order she might hear from one of Devlin Pierce's military friends. Slowly, she removed the medal and opened her hand. "I found the medal you gave to RJ. There wasn't a chain attached."

Daniel reached out and tenderly took the item into his hand. He turned it over to see his initials. "I thought it would protect him like it protected me."

Gretchen's heart was breaking for him. His lowered head was all she could see. "You are an amazing man to care so much for those boys."

"No," he whispered. "I owe them. I receive so much more from all of them than I can ever give." Finally, his head raised. His eyes were filled with tears. "His mother needs this."

"Can't you use it to prove something, anything? He was a good kid."

Daniel shrugged. "Just because you wear a medal doesn't mean anything. Trust me, I know. I'm beginning to think this medal is bad luck."

Gretchen touched his arm. "But it protected you, didn't it? Mrs. Fremont said you were a Navy pilot."

Daniel pulled away. A buzzing noise filled the apartment. Their food had arrived. Daniel almost ran to the door. "Tell them I'm coming down." He was gone before she could stop him. The precious medal remained on the counter. It stayed there until after dinner, and then it was picked up and placed in the detective's pocket without another word about it or his life.

Chapter Thirteen

Monday mornings always left Daniel Williams with a churning stomach and waiting for the other shoe to drop. With as much as Gretchen had learned, maybe it would be a stiletto. This was the first day of a stomach creating an ulcer with a week to go before the event on Saturday night. He studied his computer screen. He heard his name mentioned at one of the other desks in the room. He looked up to see a man headed his way.

"Detective Williams?" The tall man in dark navy dress pants, a light blue dress shirt, and a blue and navy striped tie extended his very tanned hand as he arrived at the desk. "I'm Agent Devlin Pierce. It's nice to meet you in person."

"It's good to have you here. Pull up a chair." Williams heard the buzz within the room. The DEA was in the house, and the agent looked like he could command the mightiest soldiers in the baddest places on earth.

"I thought you could scope out a couple of locations with me today. The rest of my team comes in tomorrow, but I wanted to get your perspective first. I hate reading reports from officers who don't have anything invested in the situation."

Williams understood, but he knew better about the police force and his brothers and sisters in arms. "I doubt if you find a more dedicated bunch of men and women, Agent Pierce. All of us live in the city, and we care about these kids. But, I'll admit, sometimes we don't see the forest for the trees."

Pierce smiled. "I get it, and sometimes there's just not the resources to do a thorough investigation. We are here to help."

Daniel sighed. "We can go now if you want. I'm not getting anything done in the office."

Pierce stood up and clapped his hands once. "Good. I was hoping you'd say that. Besides, I really need a good cup of coffee."

An hour and two cups of caffeine later, Agent Pierce and Detective Williams survey the alley one more time.

"...And then the event planner in charge of the event found a woman's nail and a medal in this alley. Up there," Daniel commented as he pointed up to the wall of the parking garage, "she found a key. We think it matches one for the store's safe. She's seen one of the corporate heads use one similar."

Pierce crouched down on the asphalt and looked up. "The planner found them? Didn't the forensic team canvas the area?"

"They did. I sent that report to you. This is the woman I was telling you about who has a knack for seeing things that some of us professionals just think are ordinary."

Dev pushed a piece of tarp around with his hand. "I know someone like that, in fact, I married her. She was a florist here in Kansas City. She's like a dog with a bone. She won't let anything go if she thinks she can figure out the puzzle."

Williams bent over to see what the agent was picking at. "Florist? Did she used to provide flowers for weddings?"

"Lots."

"I bet she knew the planner."

"What's her name?"

"Gretchen Malloy."

Dev gulped. "Gretchen? Gretchen found the evidence?"

Daniel stood up. "Have you heard of her?"

Dev joined him. "Heard of her? I have nightmares about her."

Daniel chuckled. "You really do know her. She used to, well, she still can give me a headache."

Dev touched his arm. "Gretchen is the woman you were telling me about?" Williams nodded. "I know you said she knew things, but, wait, you're **the** detective? You're the one she's been dating?"

Daniel kicked at a rock. "I wouldn't call it dating. I'm not sure what you call it when you're both over a certain age."

"I believe you still call it dating, Williams," Dev answered. His grin faded as he continued to look over the alley. "This is the perfect dumping place with no security cameras while the store was being overhauled." Dev pointed to two lights and two cameras. "These will be good for the event?"

"Yes, in fact, Gretchen is demanding to see them in action before the event. We're looking at the security company. Also, we're investigating that corporate manager. Her name is Elana Marcus. She's from Texas. Her brother is in federal prison for fraud, money laundering, and illegal substances across state lines."

"Does Gretchen know about this woman?"

"No, but she's suspicious of her. I can tell she doesn't trust her. In fact, when Gretchen is performing her sleuthing, I don't believe she trusts anyone. Everyone's a suspect. I think I am on her list too."

Dev shook his head. "That's Gretchen. My wife and she used to have their own unlicensed, unsanctioned private investigating team. On occasion, it has gotten them into a lot of trouble. I prefer to think that Lily is the sane one."

Williams bent over in laughter. "So, Lily is your wife? This is unbelievable.

Dev Pierce put on his sunglasses. He'd seen enough and had gauged where they needed to move agents. "Let's not tell Gretchen I'm in town."

"Agreed. She'll think you're here to recruit her for the DEA."

Dev began to walk away when he spotted a small piece of paper by the back door of the building. He bent down and picked up a small piece of paper. "Detective, this could be nothing, but it's a receipt from a gas station in Johnson County."

"Okay. It's helpful that you know the area. Let me look at it."

After Dev handed it off, he examined the other door to the small jewelry store. He looked up. The department's store location could make it a prime target for theft. At four-stories high, the building was one of the shortest at this edge of the Plaza. The large street in front was always bustling with traffic, but not as congested as the rest of the area. Anyone attempting escape would have instant access to almost five other thoroughfares. One path even linked up to a trafficway which could place a speeding vehicle onto a major interstate in minutes.

"Pierce, a credit card number and date are visible. It's the same date of the first murder dump. I'll see if we can access the gas station's cameras. You never know. We might get lucky."

As they walked back to the detective's car, Dev shared his thoughts. "I took a look at both coroner reports. Both were indecisive and ambiguous, but my guys did see a few things. Tito and RJ were both killed somewhere else and dropped. Tito was beaten to death. His bones were broken prior to the drop. Maybe he never revealed the information he wanted to share with your gang unit. He had been onto something about a courier which aligns with the suspicions about the diamond trade. RJ overdosed, but the scarring was consistent with someone forcing the drugs on him. The DEA considers both to be homicides."

By the time Williams started the car, Pierce added more damning information. "And I do believe your family's company is involved. Not in the way you think, but there's an obvious connection. There's chatter about a shipment of drugs coming through Kansas City this weekend. We're hearing the payment will be in diamonds. The FBI has information, and I want you to go with me tomorrow. By the way, I've already cleared it with your superiors, and you're with the DEA this week as our liaison."

Daniel nodded as he began to drive away. "Thank you. I just want justice for Tito and for RJ."

Pierce analyzed the detective. "And for yourself?"

"I suppose," Williams murmured. "Tito had such promise, and RJ was very special to me."

Dev could see that. It was always a predicament, not to mention a hard balance between your job and your humanity. You'd run into a child who touched your heart, and you couldn't do enough to make sure that victim was safe or vindicated.

"Hey Williams, turn around. I'll treat you to a burger at the most well-known place on the Plaza. I haven't been there since my wedding day, and I'd love one of their milkshakes."

"I know the place. I'll fill you in on my family's business affiliations too."

Dev Pierce admired the scenery. He used to run these streets in the early morning hours when he was assigned to a drug case that changed his life. He met Lily, fell in love with her, and eventually married the overly organized florist. He'd also taken her away from her city and her business. As they passed the hotel where he had stayed and had held their wedding reception, he smiled. Just a few years had certainly turned his world upside down.

"I would like to hear about that, but I'm more interested in how you ended up being friends, or whatever you are with Gretchen Malloy. You need to know we call her a terrorist in stilettos."

Daniel's booming laughter filled the car. "That's similar to what I've called her. Does she know your nickname for her?"

Dev grimaced. "I'm not sure. I haven't called her that to her face. Frankly, I don't have a death wish."

Before Dev Pierce called it a night, he called his wife to update her on his first day in Kansas City. "And Abby has planted a tree in the front yard of the house. Her display window looks great, and she seems to be doing well with the shop."

"That's nice to hear," Lily mumbled. Dev had forgotten it was an hour later in Virginia. "Before I forget, will you pick up my favorite barbecue sauce?"

"I already have it in my bag. Have you talked to Gretchen lately?"

Lily yawned. "She texted me the other day. She's dating a cop. Are you going to see her?"

Dev found a hockey game on his hotel room's television. "Not if I can help it."

Lily chuckled. "Why not, Mr. Delicious?"

Dev cringed. "And that's exactly why I'm not making it a priority. By the way, that cop is the detective who is working with us."

"Seriously?"

"What kind of man is he?"

How much should I tell Lily? "He seems to be a good guy. He's younger than her, in his forties maybe, and he's divorced." Dev stopped. *I don't have to tell my wife everything, do I?*

"Devlin, what else? I can hear you're not telling me something."

"Geez, Lily. I wasn't saying anything."

Lily knew her husband. "Spill."

Dev shook his head. "You have to promise that you won't tell her. I mean it."

Lily wasn't as tired as she was when her husband had called. Her interest was definitely piqued. "He isn't a criminal mastermind, right? Wait, she'd probably be okay with that. I promise I won't tell her, but it's going to kill me."

"Just don't talk to her until after Saturday's event," Dev suggested. "He has money, lots of it, and she doesn't know. He has his own plane, and his family owns a world-renowned diamond company."

Lily hit the bed where Dev should be reclining. "She's hit the jackpot."

"Lily, I mean it. You can't tell her."

Someone should tell her! "Fine, but I can't believe she doesn't know it already. She knows everything. Besides, why would she be with him?"

"She likes him, and he likes her," Dev admitted.

"It won't last," Lily lamented. "With Gretchen it doesn't last more than a night."

"Don't you always tell me that anything is possible with love? Just look at us." Dev smirked knowing he'd used her own logic to rebuke her. "I plan on being home as soon as I can."

Now, Lily swept her hand softly over his pillow. "That would be nice." She paused. "Don't use my logic against me, but you're right. No one has a bigger heart than Gretchen Malloy. It would be lovely to see her happy in every part of her life. I think she's been lonely since that past love of her life came back and then left again."

Dev understood completely. He never knew he needed Lily until he didn't have her. He knew how you could be happy being alone and on your own, but then you'd meet that person, and you just couldn't even walk around your house without thinking of that insanely organized florist back in Kansas City. Lily yawned again.

"Honey, I'll call you when I can. Go to sleep. I love you, Lily."

"Love you. Good night."

The last thing he heard was a long yawn. It was time to call it a night. This

week could be full of surprises. If he made a list of what could happen, Gretchen's heart breaking wouldn't even make the top ten.

Chapter Fourteen

"Putnam, what do you have for me?" Gretchen demanded. Here it was the morning of her event, and she had no more information on what she might expect to happen, or what had happened to Tito and RJ.

"The police know more than they're telling everyone. The first kid was abducted by a van. They have footage where he was taken from his job."

"The van had Control Systems Security on the side, right?" Gretchen continued to pack her bag for this evening's event. She threw in a pair of flats just in case her feet failed her.

The reporter puffed on his cigar. "How do you know this stuff? I had to bribe somebody."

"I keep telling you I know everything and everyone in this town. What else do you have?"

"There's a rumor that those diamonds are hot."

Gretchen hit her bathroom counter. "You are nuts. They are not hot. I saw the collection last night, and believe me buddy, I know my diamonds. They are being held in a bank vault, and I'm not telling you which one. Elana and I saw them. Besides, this is a big deal. That diamond company is one of the best in the world. But, did you find anything on Elana?"

"Not much, but I do know they have been looking at her. There's some big DEA guy and his team in town. But why or how your event, a drug case, and the diamonds are all connected is above my pay scale. What does your detective think?"

I don't know. I can't read him. He baffles me. "I've been too busy to deal with him. He does his thing, and I do mine."

Putnam bit his cigar. "Trouble in paradise? Is your little fling over?"

"We aren't having a fling," Gretchen lied.

"Yell at me when you want a real man, Malloy."

"And you'll find me one?" Gretchen taunted.

The reporter coughed. "I was talking about myself."

Gretchen bit her tongue. *What a sad little man.* "Let me know if you have any more information. I have you on the guest list so watch for anything. If you can possibly behave like a normal human being, I'll make sure you get that interview with Marty in just a couple of weeks."

"That's in addition to what we agreed on for the night before the election, right? I want to run it on my social media."

"Yes, yes. I have to go. See you tonight, weasel."

Putnam smirked. "Weasel? Fine. Then you're my stiletto fiend."

By the time Gretchen arrived at the store, the florists were finishing up the decor. The store brought in their own crew from Miami. *I wish Abby were here. She'd keep me calm.*

Gretchen drew in a deep breath, smiled, stood erect as she could, and found Elana. "I'm here. What can I do?"

"The ice sculpture arrives in a bit, but I need you to go over the schedule one more time with the caterer. I'm finishing with the florists."

Gretchen shrugged. "Of course. I wish you'd use a couple of florists I know in Kansas City. Their flowers are gorgeous, and I just like to have a family feeling with my vendors."

Elana's smile faded quickly. "You chose the caterer. I didn't want them. I feel better with my own people. In fact, we really didn't need you. The charity pushed you on me."

Gretchen was completely blindsided. This warning shot was more like a full-on attack across the bridge. *Where is her anger coming from?* "Elana, I won't be talked to like this. I'm a professional, and I thought you were as well."

The workers doing various jobs around the store had stopped when they heard the yelling. Elana planted a large smile on her face. "Everything is fine. I'm just a little nervous." She took Gretchen by the hand and led her to the presentation area for the red diamonds. They were alone in that area.

"What the hell was that?" Gretchen asked.

"I'm so sorry. I'm not used to having someone hold my hand through an opening. I've been stressed all day. I apologize. I didn't mean any of that."

Gretchen studied the young woman. She seemed uncontrollably nervous. She literally was sweating, and it was cool in the store. "Have the florists been a problem? You seem to be bothered about them?"

"No, of course not. Everything is fine. I'm not used to using local vendors, that's all. I never expressed that to you, and I just lost it. Again, I apologize. You've been a jewel. I'm not sure I could've pulled it all together without you." Elana reached over to offer a brief hug. "We need to get back to work. You just do your thing."

As Elana briskly walked away to speak with one of the florists, Gretchen watched in disbelief. As if she didn't think something was up before with this event, now she knew it. Elana went straight up to the top of her suspect list.

Gretchen wouldn't dismiss it as just nerves, but she decided to continue doing her own preparations. By the time four men carrying the enormous artwork of an ice champagne glass entered the store, Gretchen was in control. It was placed in the middle of the room on a large round table. One man climbed a ladder to carefully drop a bowl of cubic zirconia into the very top of the sculpture. Elana stood below the worker, handing him another bowl of fake diamonds. They were barely seen from the rim of the ice sculpture.

Elana smiled over at Gretchen. "It will be perfect when the guests arrive."

"It will be stunning," Gretchen agreed. "I'm so happy you decided not to put the real diamonds in there."

"I thought it was a cool idea, but you were right. Our insurance underwriters thought I was crazy."

Gretchen touched her arm. "One of my first rules is to never take a chance. If we even lost one diamond, both of us wouldn't have a job."

Elana pulled away. The sweet smile and tone in her voice had vanished very quickly. Gretchen eyed her as she walked back into the offices. "Something is off with you." *Diamonds? Does Elana have something to do with the priceless gems? Maybe it's a heist.* She quickly texted Putnam her suspicions. Gretchen looked up at the faux gems. *Does cubic zirconia really sparkle like that?*

Gretchen was uncomfortable. She looked to the back of the store and saw an open door. She could see the alley. She strode determinedly and peeked her head outside. At the end of the lane was a Control System Security van. She headed carefully to the vehicle, removed her phone and took photos. She captured all sides of the van, the license plate. When she shot the interior, she saw a piece of hot pink material, similar to a scarf. She also saw some sort of powder. In the console she saw a small bottle of nail polish. *It's Fruity-Tutti, Tutti-Fruity, oh hell! It's that color! That trapeze girl wore that scarf when I met her, and that powder could be resin. Larkin is involved, and why is she in that security van?*

Gretchen needed to do something. But what if she was wrong? She looked around to check out the newly installed cameras. *If I just go around to the other side, anyone seeing that footage will just think I've gone down the block? I could talk my way out of it.*

Gretchen had a plan. It was an older van. The tires look like they had a few miles on them. Quickly, she went back into the store and grabbed her bag. She ran past the caterers who were complaining about the vehicle blocking that edge of the alley. "I have to get some flowers. I'll be back." She waved at the chef she knew as she passed.

The premier event planner ran down the block and purchased a bouquet of flowers. She'd offer them to Elana in thanks. *Elana will believe it. Lily never would.* She hurried out of the flower shop and ran back to the van. Two men in a convertible whistled at her as she rounded the corner to the alley.

"No time, boys!" she yelled back.

Gretchen looked at the tires. She pretended to drop the bouquet and crouched down. She removed a wipe out of her bag, and pulled out an ice pick. She had a corkscrew too, but it must've fallen into the bottom. She stood up with flowers in hand and pretended to notice something on the ground. With the sharp implement in hand, she punctured both tires. It took strength to plunge the pick in, but it was an added challenge to remove it. *I guess the yoga and kickboxing classes actually come in handy.* She stood up calmly. *It's done. You never know when you'll need an ice pick.* For many a wedding, it did come in handy at an outside bar. She also carried a spare silver-plated knife just in case there was a cake to be cut, and the corkscrew to open any nearby bottle of wine.

With hands cleaned, wipes thrown away, ice pick in the bag, smoothed hair, and deep breath, Gretchen was ready. She handed the flowers to Elana. "I think you are a marvelous woman. These are for you as a thank you."

Elana's face burned red. "Thank you. I did enjoy working with you, but I've been so worried."

"Can I help you? What can I do, no matter what?" Gretchen whispered.

Elana shook her head, but Gretchen could see the distress on her face. It wasn't just nerves. "No. It's all on me.

Do me a favor, when the aerialist begins her spotlighted routine where she dips her cup into the ice sculpture to pull out the diamonds, could you make sure no one is standing right below? We don't want a guest to be hit in the eye with a gem."

"I've done one better," Gretchen replied. "I have the area roped off. I try to think of every scenario." *Except whatever you're hiding!*

"It seems like everything is under control." Elana sauntered away, enjoying the fragrance of her gifted flowers.

It's all under control until all hell breaks loose, and I have no idea what is coming or what I'm going to do when it happens.

Chapter Fifteen

"Oh my!" Gretchen's eyes strained to see the practicing aerialist hanging in the air. "No way in–"

She felt lips kissing her neck softly. Seldom did she wear her hair up, but tonight was a special event. *This is worth the choice I made!*

"Hello, beautiful."

Gretchen closed her eyes as she turned slowly. It was him. The timbre of voice could calm her and make her head go empty of any thoughts. It rumbled through her soul and made her toes curl. Once again, she was swept off balance by him. She opened her eyes and saw his crooked smile. "Good evening, Detective Williams."

"Good evening, Ms. Malloy." He eyed her up and down. She was stunning in a charcoal gray evening jumpsuit with flowing sleeves and pants. On her feet tonight she wore jeweled stilettos.

Gretchen took a couple of steps back to examine her assistant for the evening. "That tux isn't a rental."

"You said to wear a tux. You said it was black tie, and you wanted me here early. I'm in a tux, and I'm early."

Gretchen's eyes roamed. "Those shoes have to be yours. Are they comfortable?"

"Yes, very. Why does that matter?"

Gretchen smiled. "Ah hah! If they hurt, they are rentals. That tux fits too well. What detective do you know who owns his own tuxedo and the shoes to match?"

"The ones on television?" Daniel chuckled. "Seriously, I had it hanging in my closet, and it just screamed to be worn. Satisfied?"

"Yes. You are so dear to be with me tonight."

"As I recall, I'm the one who wanted the invitation."

Gretchen bridged the space between him and felt his very clean-shaven face. "It does matter that you're here. You make an old girl feel like a teenager."

Daniel soothed a loose tendril of her hair. He kissed her cheek, murmuring against her face. "You have the energy of a teenager. You are more beautiful than anyone I've ever seen. Besides, when have you ever felt old?"

"Tonight. There's something very wrong." Gretchen searched his eyes. "I think Elana, the young lady from corporate, is involved in a heist."

"Okay."

Gretchen pulled away. "You don't seem surprised. Detective?"

Daniel glanced up. "Wow. The sculpture is beautiful. Those aren't real diamonds are they?" He walked closer to gain a better look.

"No, silly. I talked Elana out of using the real ones. That would be a nightmare, and the underwriters agreed with me."

"Of course she wanted the real ones," Daniel muttered as he attempted to examine the gems. "So what is she going to do with them?" He pointed up at Larkin.

"She's going to dip the cup into the top of the glass, pretend to be drinking, and then she'll spill some gems out. It's all very artsy. Don't worry, we'll keep the guests out of the target zone."

Daniel texted quickly with his back to Gretchen. "And what about the security for the real diamonds?"

"The diamond company brought in their own guards at the last minute. Do you know that the security company that put the cameras in the alley has their van parked back there?" *And that I hopefully disabled two of their tires? I'll tell him later, if it comes to that.*

The detective glanced over at the special showing area for the main event diamonds. "How did she get up there? I don't see a staging area."

"They installed a removable skylight. Once this event has concluded, they'll secure it. She came down through a four-floor open area. I love the design, don't you?"

"So, did she drop down from the roof?"

Gretchen's eyes narrowed. "They put her up on the roof an hour ago via a cherry picker. Daniel, did you bring your gun?"

Daniel nodded.

Gretchen moved around him so she could look into his eyes. Those gray beauties were clouds of gray. They were also dark tonight as though a thunderstorm was coming.

She took his right hand in hers, and he looked down at the action. "Daniel, something is going to happen, isn't it?"

"Yes, a lovely event." He softened his gaze quickly. *She's beginning to read me just like Agent Pierce said happened with him and his wife.*

"Daniel, please, just be honest with me this one time."

She was pleading with her eyes. He hated this. "Gretchen, we have it all under control. The Chief okayed my gun. It seems we have plenty of security. It will be a lovely event."

Gretchen flicked a piece of lint from his lapel. "Of course. The Chief is such a sweetie. I did his daughter's wedding two years ago."

"I wouldn't exactly call him a sweetie. Maybe a hard–"

Gretchen pulled him away to a nearby counter. She filled his hands with auction programs. "This group goes up front by the registration table. I'll need another stack over by the auction items on the jewelry counter."

"I must be crazy to work for you."

"Lucky for you I love crazy." She kissed him briefly on the cheek and shoved him away. "Go and do. We're almost ready to open the doors."

After he had completed his job, he greeted the staff from his company. It was good to see a few friends again. He also texted a few more times to Agent Pierce who was busy preparing for his own mission. His last text said they were arming up and arriving at their positions.

By the time Daniel arrived back at Gretchen's side she was approving the presentation of food on a silver platter. "I've been looking around. Whose brainiac idea was it to have an event in a high-end department store with all of this jewelry?"

As soon as he saw Gretchen's look, he knew instantly. "Mine. The hospital charity needed a space for their fundraiser, and the store wanted a large splash as they reopened. Do you have any more brilliant comments?"

"No, ma'am." Gretchen's shoulders raised as though she had heard nails on a chalkboard.

"That word makes me feel like an old lady, and it certainly doesn't help when said by a younger male friend."

"I'm sorry. I'll make it up to you after this is all over. We'll do whatever you want." He pulled her into a soft embrace.

Her finger traced his mouth. *Anything?* "I'd love a couple's massage or maybe a pedicure. You would love it. They have these little fishes that eat the dead skin from your feet. You'll love it, darling!"

"And you're back. Fine. We'll go fishing." Actually, he needed a manicure. His hands had seen better days. His cuticles were a little rough. In his memories, he could hear his mother and grandmother reprimanding him for his lack of proper hygiene. They used to say the hands were a window to the soul of a man. He couldn't be a gentleman in society and have callused hands. So, he left society behind.

Gretchen patted his arm and headed for her clipboard. She took charge, and he watched. *What a force she is!*

Chapter Sixteen

With the servers in place, the caterer and musicians ready, Gretchen gave the order to open the doors. Guests streamed in and began to marvel at the improvements to the store. They headed to the counters to view the auction items.

"This could be a record-breaking event," Elana commented as she came to Gretchen's side.

"That would be wonderful." Gretchen nudged Elana. "I forgot to introduce you two. This is Elana, Elana this is Detective Williams."

As soon as his name had fallen from her lips, Gretchen realized her mistake. Elana's eyes widened, and she didn't take Daniel's hand as he presented it. Daniel watched the woman's face flush. "I'm just here to help Ms. Malloy, and I wanted to see all those real pretty diamonds over there. It's really fancy. I've never been to anything like this big shindig. It's really nice to meet a lady like you. Do you think I could bid about fifty dollars and get those football tickets?"

Elana's smile softened her face. "Unfortunately, the bid for December's game tickets is already over five hundred dollars, detective. But you enjoy your night. Gretchen, I'll see you later."

"And what game are you playing, Detective Williams?" Gretchen murmured. "It's a fancy shindig? Fifty dollars? You have a tux hanging in your closet."

"She lowered her expectations of me, didn't she?"

Gretchen laughed. "I hope you have a wonderful night at this fancy event." She turned on her heels and began to head to a former client.

"It will be a night to remember."

Gretchen's heels stopped clicking. She coyly turned her head, batting her very fake eyelashes. "Why detective, are you talking about the event or much later in the privacy of my boudoir?"

"Gretchen, stop that. I'm going to get a drink." He began to walk away, but instead came to her side once more. He leaned in and whispered, "Later tonight."

His low voice sent shivers down her back, nice shivers that made her wish it was already much later. "Holy Moly."

The event was a hit. The quartet's music was just right. The large area between the counters was filled with conversations and laughter. Several ladies were shopping, many others were placing bids. Gretchen spied Daniel looking over one of the items. It was a trip to the Bahamas.

She looked over his right shoulder. "Are you planning a trip?"

"Do you need to know everything, Ms. Malloy, supreme busybody?"

"Actually I do, especially tonight. I'm still worried about what might happen."

Williams picked up a pen and placed a bid. Her face neared his to see what amount of money he had marked. "Do you mind? I'm trying to win a trip here."

"Why?"

He finished writing quickly to block her view. "Because I'd like to help the charity. I'm starving. Let's get something to eat. I saw shrimp somewhere."

"I do know everything, and I can prove it. The shrimp are right over there. I'm hungry too."

The food stations were strategically placed throughout the store, but the shrimp cocktail was just past the private viewing area for the red diamonds. Gretchen looked longingly at the area.

"You know, they're just pieces of carbon," Williams commented. "You're salivating."

"The shrimp are excellent." Gretchen acted unphased.

Daniel chuckled. "I'm not talking about the food, and you know it. Why don't we just walk in, and you can see those magical red diamonds?"

"Because some of them go for millions of dollars, and I can't afford it. Although, they are in my color. I'm not sure I'd be able to breathe, Daniel."

Williams captured her small plate and stacked it on his, handing them off to a passing server. He grasped her hand and began to tug. "You'll be able to breathe. Come on."

"We can't."

"We can, and we will. Come on, Gretchen. You're the one who lives in the fast lane. Let's go see a red diamond and tell everyone they do exist. We may even see a unicorn. It's a magical night."

They were both waved in quickly. "Daniel, did you bribe those security guards? You need a reservation."

The detective walked with purpose to the last table at the farthest end of the room. "We have one. There he is. Besides, you're not the only one with connections, Ms. Malloy."

"Mr. Williams and Ms. Malloy, I have the diamonds for your review."

Upon a velvet palette as though they were from the Queen, lay six amazing red diamonds in varying sizes and color. Gretchen averted her eyes. It was just too painful. "Daniel, this isn't funny. You are hurting my very soul."

"Gretchen, it never hurts to look."

His order shook her. She pulled away from his grasp as she stamped her foot. "This isn't funny. I mean it. It does hurt to just look and know one of those beauties won't be coming home with me."

Daniel took both of her hands and held them in front of them. "Let's pretend that I can afford one of them. They're your signature color, for heaven's sake. Which one would you choose?"

"We are wasting this man's time. All they have to do is check your credit, and they'll discover you're a fraud."

"Wow, that was extremely harsh, even for you. I didn't know you could be so judgemental."

Gretchen scoffed at the charade. *Is he trying to break it off with me? This is sad.* She pulled her hands from his and stepped back. "I've never been so humiliated. Daniel, please stop."

The gentleman presenting the stones extended a hand to the seats in front of the counter. "There's really no harm in just looking at something so beautiful, Ms. Malloy."

Unconvinced, but one who really wanted to see those diamonds, Gretchen slowly sat down as though she was sitting down to tea with the pope. "I suppose there's no harm in just looking."

Daniel clapped his hands and sat down next to her. "Which one really speaks to you?"

Gretchen grabbed one of the loops off of the counter and began to meticulously examine each red stone. "My. They are exquisite. There's a few flaws in a couple of them, but who would know?"

Daniel shared a look with the jeweler. He marveled at Gretchen. She was as exquisite as the gems. Fiery, cut perfectly with just a couple of flaws that one could overlook because those imperfections made her who she was, Gretchen was in her element. With age, just like those pieces of carbon, she became better and worth more than just the simple value of what one could see on the exterior.

"If I were ever able to purchase one of these, this would be the one."

Daniel followed Gretchen's finger. "Why that one? It isn't the largest, and it isn't perfect."

"As you've reminded me since I've met you, perfect isn't always the best. We all have our flaws, don't we? This one does speak to me."

Gretchen was too giddy from the experience to notice Daniel's nod to the presenter. "Wasn't that fun?" He received a glare as an answer.

"It was about as much fun as having a perfectly grilled steak on your plate and you have no teeth." She smiled sweetly at the jeweler and stood up quickly. "Thank you. It was lovely to review those amazing diamonds. Daniel, I must go back to work now."

She turned on her heels before Daniel could detain her. He turned back to the presenter. "Make sure you watch everyone, and I mean everyone, Ferrity. Pull half of the inventory right now and send it out to the vault. No one will realize we have stock missing."

"Yes, sir. I did increase our security, and I trust these men with my life. None of our diamonds are out in the store. There was a woman from Laurent's who was rather nosy. I refused to tell her anything."

"That would be Elana. She's one of our suspects. Good man. How is my mother?"

Ferrity smiled. "Feisty as ever, much like the woman you're with."

Daniel's shoulders flinched. "Please don't say that. It's every man's nightmare to think he's attracted to someone like his mother."

"Yes, sir, but if I might say, your friend has excellent taste in diamonds and in company. It is so good to see you again."

Daniel reached over the velvet palette to shake his hand. "I have missed seeing you, my friend. I'll be back for the board meeting. Now, get those diamonds out of here."

Chapter Seventeen

Williams checked his phone. Agent Pierce wasn't texting or responding. The DEA's operation was underway. Outside of the department store, he knew the police were in place. Daniel looked up to see Gretchen speaking with the mayor and his wife. He gazed up at the young woman hanging upside down like a bat. She was about twenty feet from the ice sculpture. As he searched the room for anything that looked out of the ordinary, he noticed Elana pacing back and forth by the customer service area of the store. She had a plastered smile on her face, but the shaking of her hands gave her away. Suddenly, a security guard's body hid her from Daniel's view. He seemed very animated as he grasped her upper arm and pushed her out of his sight.

Once Gretchen moved away from the mayor, Daniel joined her. "Elana is upset by something, and a guard has her in the back area."

"Is he from Control Systems Security? If he is, he's bad news," Gretchen muttered.

"He is. You gave me all your notes, but I still feel the need to interrogate you."

Gretchen grabbed his lapels and smiled. "Oh, Daniel, that could be fun. I particularly enjoy a good search, but I don't have the time. Maybe later, darling?"

Daniel continued to watch what little he could see. The guard and Elana were still talking. "Gretchen, don't make me handcuff you. And stop licking your lips. If I have to handcuff you, it will be for your own protection and not for—"

"Something else? I could think of many activities." Gretchen patted his firm chest. "So many."

Daniel shook his head. "You're trying to distract me. What have you seen?"

Playfully, Gretchen pointed skyward and waved at Larkin. She spoke through her teeth. "Little Larkin up there knows that same guard. When I saw the bottle of nail polish, the scarf she had been wearing, and the resin in the van, I suspected her, but when the guard and she shared a knowing nod just a bit ago while I was talking with Hal, I knew."

Daniel rubbed her back as though they were sharing an intimate conversation. "What van?"

Gretchen's chin lifted in dramatic fashion. "Are you the detective now? Is that what's going on? Something is going down, isn't it?"
"You're the one who wanted me to bring my gun."

Gretchen stepped away. "It doesn't matter. I still have to keep this event going. Anytime I'm involved with you, my business is always in jeopardy."

"It's not my fault," Daniel complained. "You get yourself in these situations." Suddenly, a sharp pain passed just above his eyebrows.

"Do what you are going to do. Pardon me, but I have work to do." Gretchen purposefully glanced at his arm as she stalked toward a microphone.

Daniel winced. "That went well."

Gretchen announced the closing of one silent auction and the beginning of another. She instructed the guests to look above them. Most of the party goers gathered around the area by the ice sculpture. High above, Larkin had lowered herself in clear reach of the goblet. She held a glass of her own and after several somersaults and stretches, she dipped her glass into the top of the sculpture. Her act wasn't seamless. It seemed to take her a little longer as the cup came up to her lips.

"Gretchen isn't going to like a glitch," Daniel murmured. His eyes narrowed as he moved to the side to see what she was doing. "What is she doing?"

Suddenly, the aerialist threw out gems, many of them flying past the roped off area. Guests scrambled, ducked, and some attempted to catch what appeared to be clear diamonds.

"Those aren't genuine, folks," Daniel said out loud. He kept his gaze on the aerialist, and that's when he saw the switch. Larkin had placed a small pouch under the band of the sheer skirt she wore. "Gretchen, something is wrong. There's been a handoff."

Larkin heard him yell. She tugged at her support, and she was quickly hoisted up through the opening in the roof. Gretchen pushed through the crowd still grabbing at stones on the floor to arrive at his side.

"Daniel, those stones weren't supposed to create chaos, and Larkin had another routine to do." Gretchen looked over the guests to try to see Elana.

"Elana is gone." He pulled Gretchen close to his body. "You stay with me

from now on. I think the flying girl has a pouch of real diamonds. This is a heist of monumental proportions."

In the next seconds, shots began firing. Daniel shoved Gretchen behind a fully dressed mannequin. He pulled his gun but couldn't see where the shots were coming from. He screamed over the din of the frightened guests into his phone for assistance. He thought he heard an acknowledgement that shots had been fired.

He placed his hand on Gretchen's back. "Honey, we need to get to that van and stop them. Take me to it."

Gretchen nodded. "The back exit. The emergency door takes us directly back to the alley."

"Stay low."

As they made their way to the door, Daniel turned to glimpse the presentation area. He couldn't see Ferrity or his company's guards. Hopefully, they had left the building before all this began.

The exit was blocked by a large metal cabinet which featured one open door. "No," Gretchen screamed. "This shouldn't be here. And where are the caterers?"

Daniel looked around for any implement he could use to get out of the room or to move the blockage. "They were all out watching your entertainment, or they were serving the food."

Gretchen examined the opening. *Maybe we could tumble it over?* There was no time. A large blast from behind shoved them into the cabinet.

"What is going on out there?" he yelled. "Gretchen, you stay there."

Gretchen pulled at his lapels as he turned to leave. "Oh, no. You're not going anywhere."

"Honey, I'm a detective, and I have a gun. Let me go."

Daniel attempted to pull away, but Gretchen rocked forward to stop him. The always strong Gretchen began to shake. With the sound of another blast, Daniel fell into her while debris began to fall around them, closing the door behind them.

In complete darkness, they heard screams. Daniel shifted to Gretchen's side for a little more room. He managed to turn. In an effort to turn the latch, his fist flew up, knocking into her arm. "I'm sorry. We need to get this open." He shoved. He secured the safety on his gun and shoved the butt under the latch. It moved slightly. He was able to peek out. Another large piece of debris that looked like shelving fell and created their prison. "We're stuck now."

"It's awfully close in here," Gretchen said slowly.

Daniel placed his arm around her. "Are you claustrophobic?"

"No."

"We have air. It's still coming in through this crack. See?"

"I see. It's a very tiny crack," she answered slowly.

Daniel leaned back. There wasn't one inch of space between them. "Are you afraid of small spaces?"

"I'd rather not say."

Daniel titled his head in frustration. "Gretchen, now isn't the time to play games."

"Fine," she spat out. "We're too close. I really should be asking if that's your gun or–"

Daniel's chest shook in nervous laughter. "I'm glad to see you?"

"Something like that, but I realize it's your cell phone."

"Cell. Gretchen, reach in my pocket and get my phone."

Gretchen's hand skimmed down below his waist. "Now, you want to get romantic? You have the worst timing. Am I in the vicinity of your pocket?"

"Oh." Daniel's breath quickened. "Um, you need to move your hand a little further over, not down."

Gretchen giggled. "Oh, sorry, well, I'm not really sorry. Actually, if we ever do, well you know, could we play detective and criminal seducer? I promise it will be fun, and do bring the cuffs."

"Do you have it?" Williams growled.

Gretchen felt the phone. "I'm touching it. I mean, I have your phone."

"Good, now just hit home. You'll get emergency services."

"Got it. I'll put it on speaker."

After a brief description of where they were located and what was going on at the event, Daniel and Gretchen were assured that the operation was underway around the exterior of the store and even in the store itself. When the call ended, they were thrown into darkness once more.

Daniel could hear Gretchen's breathing. It seemed stressed. "I still have a full battery if you want to have light."

"I'm better in the dark," she whispered.

"As long as we're stuck in here, I might as well ask you something I'm always wondering. Why do you make everything so, well so–"

"So me?"

Daniel stretched his neck to no avail. "That's not exactly where I was going, but okay, so you?"

"I'm in love with every aspect of life. Romance, lust, and lovemaking are very important parts of life. Besides, I absolutely adore men. They seem to like me too, but you are so different. You have this control, this mystique that I can't figure out. If you aren't attracted to me, I understand. There are those few sad men who miss out on my many skills."

"I am very attracted to you."

The cabinet interior was starkly quiet. No quips or witty retorts filled the air. "Then, why haven't you tried–"

"To spend the night?"

Gretchen nodded even though Daniel couldn't see. She bent her head back on his chest. "It really is the age difference, isn't it? I realize you have a station in this community."

Daniel shifted his arm awkwardly, pushing up against the side of their vault and across her back. "For the final time, it isn't your age or mine. I know women half your age who aren't as alive as you. You're intelligent, witty, very sexual, communicative, and frankly, you're the whole package. Except for those heels. I can always hear you before I see you. And do you know you drum your fingernails when you're nervous? I have my reasons for taking my time, and I guess you'd say I was a little old fashioned. And I'm not a prude."

"You think I'm very sexual?" Gretchen purred. "I just remembered I'm mad at you. You know more about what is going on out there than you have shared."

Silence was again trapped inside with them.

"Daniel, you know we could occupy ourselves."

Her companion flexed his right leg. "It's quiet out there. Do you hear anything?"

"Your beating heart. Daniel, as long as we're in this teeny, tiny space–"

"Can you breathe okay?"

Gretchen smelled smoke. "Oh Lord. There's a fire. We'll melt in here."

Daniel brought his hand down to her shoulders. "They know we're back here. We're going to be fine."

"Just my luck. I'm going to die with a man at my side, but not with a satisfied smile on my face."

"Gretchen, take nice, easy breaths. Don't pant."

"I pant when I'm nervous, and when…I'm sorry. I won't talk about that."

Daniel patted her shoulder. "Good. Don't even think about that."

Gretchen hit his body with her hand. "You do think we'll die here, don't you? I'm always prepared, but I didn't have this on my list of things to do. I'm sorry. If I had my bag, we could maybe use that icepick."

Daniel closed his eyes. *An icepick? Note to self, check her bag for grenades.*

Gretchen sighed. "Oh no. You aren't in my will. What am I thinking? You'll be dead too. Lily is going to be so upset when she hears I'm gone. She may fall into a pit of depression. Abby will make the most beautiful casket spray. I can see it now. She'll use orchids in all shades. Wait, what if she doesn't know I love orchids?"

"It won't matter. You won't be there," Daniel grumbled. He struggled to throw off his bow tie, unbuttoning his shirt. Several studs flew off and hit the metal.

"I will be there. I'll be the most fantastic spirit. Yes, a spirit in stilettos. I wonder if that's been done before?"

Daniel banged his head on the cabinet. "Who knows or cares? And no, it hasn't."

Gretchen smiled in the darkness. "I will be the first spirit in stilettos."

Daniel laughed uncontrollably. He couldn't wipe the tears from his eyes.

"What's so funny?"

"I just thought about God and you. He doesn't have a chance. If there's a file on you, he'll probably just send it flying after about five minutes of one of your stories. I know, you'll say, Lord, I would've been here earlier, but there was this sailor. He and I ate oysters by the bay while the sun set into the water. We went skinny dipping, and then we returned to our room for hours of lovemaking with peanut butter–"

"Have I told you that story before?" Gretchen questioned.

Daniel laughed louder. "Stop. I can't breathe. I was making it up."

"No, there really was a sailor, and we used peanut butter–"

"Stop. I don't want to know." He paused briefly. He needed to distract her until they found them. "Did you ever think about having a family?"

"I had a family," Gretchen bit back.

"I mean children of your own."

Gretchen attempted to take in a deep breath but failed. "Of course. Time passed. I was busy and successful. The men I briefly loved came in and out of my life. No one seemed to stay."

Williams nodded. "I understand. I married my ex-wife a few years out of college. Her career took off like a rocket."

"What did she do?"

"Actually, you'd like her. She's a fashion designer living in Paris. We were living in New York City, and I wanted a baby, but she didn't. Then on a beautiful September morning, I went to work in lower Manhattan. The sky was so blue that day, until it wasn't. I heard the planes. By eleven that morning, our entire world crumbled, literally. It was the day the planes hit the World Trade buildings. We couldn't go back to our apartment so we went to live with my mother in Massachusetts. And that was the beginning of the end of our marriage."

"Oh, Daniel. That day was awful."

The detective sighed. It seemed like a lifetime ago, but he could still smell the debris, the jet fuel, and the death. "I lost friends and family."

"Is that why you went into law enforcement?"

Daniel searched his mind for an accurate answer. "Maybe, but I felt the need to do something. My wife just wanted it all to go back to the way it had been on September tenth, but nothing could be the same on September twelfth. A few acquaintances enlisted, but I continued to fight the feeling until New Year's Eve. My wife handed me a glass of champagne. She complained I wasn't acting like myself, and she wasn't happy. She also informed me she was having an affair with a college friend."

"No," Gretchen muttered. "She did it on New Year's Eve?"

Daniel chuckled. "It gets better. The party was at the guy's house. His wife didn't know either."

"Wow, that's almost better than some of my stories. What did you do?"

"At one minute until midnight, my wife touched my glass with hers and said she wanted a divorce. I wouldn't provide the lifestyle she desperately needed. I drank my champagne. I remember placing the glass on a tray, and I walked out. I passed the friend, and I told him to tell his wife. That was the last time I saw any of those bores and fakes. I enlisted in the Navy the next week. I knew how to fly so they taught me how to do it off of an aircraft carrier."

"I know a Navy SEAL," Gretchen said proudly.

"Of course you do, Gretchen."

"I'm sorry you never had your family, Daniel." The empathy in her voice warmed his heart. "Is that why RJ meant so much to you?"

The woman understood him. "They are my kids. I don't know what I'd do without them."

"Daniel Williams, you are probably one of the best men I have ever known."

Silence engulfed them once more.

"Shouldn't there be alarms and sprinklers going off?" Gretchen wondered.

"Yes. That's weird."

Gretchen had her suspicions. "Not if Control Systems Security was in charge of the installation."

"But they're checked by the fire chief before any business opens. At some point they were working." Daniel felt the shelves that trapped them shift slightly against the door. Hopefully his companion didn't realize.

"I'm going to miss Marty winning his senate race."

"No, you won't. But he could lose."

Gretchen shook her head in protest. "He will not."

Daniel coughed and cleared his throat. "Chance will be back, won't he?"

"I suppose." Gretchen's voice was barely audible. "His daughter had a girl. I talked to Marty the other day, and Chance's team has been working for a few weeks now."

"Do you still love Chance?"

"Do you still love your ex-wife?" Gretchen asked quickly.

"Honestly, I will always love her in some way, but I wouldn't want to remarry her, if that's what you're asking. What about Chance?"

"I've always loved Chance, but I don't need or want him in my life. I haven't for many years now. We made our choices, and we have lived them."

"But, do you want to get back with him?"

"Oh, no." Gretchen was very decisive about that. She never had dreams of Chance riding into the sunset with her. Chance wanted his rocking chair; Gretchen wanted a fast car.

"Are you absolutely sure about that?" For some reason, Daniel Williams needed to hear her say something more definitive.

"Yes. You don't know Chance like I do. Years ago, we were so young, but we both knew what we wanted and needed. He joined the Marines. He told me we would marry and roam the world together, while I stayed behind, and he deployed to wherever. I wanted to be asked and consulted. I wanted an honest discussion. That wasn't his style then, and I fear it still isn't. I like my freedom, Daniel."

"So, that's it? Gretchen is always free, and she never wants to be caught?"

Gretchen thought for a second. "I'm a free spirit, but if I were running in sneakers, I think I might let you catch me. But don't ever put me in a box. Oh, Daniel, we're going to die here. It's getting harder to breathe." Gretchen began to sob. Her shaking shoulders were held by Daniel's arm.

"Get it together. Conserve the air. Breathe in and out. Come on Ms. Malloy, you will live another day to buy a new pair of high heels."

"Do you promise, Daniel?"

"A wise man once told me to always tell you yes. So, yes, Gretchen, I promise. Heck, I'll buy those killer stilettos for you."

Barely able to reach her eyes, Gretchen swiped at her one cheek and then the other. "That's the sweetest thing to say. You called my stilettos killers."

"Gretchen. Gretchen." Someone was calling her, and it wasn't Daniel.

"Holy Moly, Daniel. God is calling me. Did you hear? Of course not. He's calling me."

"Gretchen. Gretchen."

Daniel heard the voice nearing the cabinet. "I hear the voice too."

"Oh, no. We're going to die like two Egyptian royals trapped in a tomb. It's romantic but terribly sad."

The file cabinet began to shake. "Gretchen, are you in here?"

Daniel recognized the voice. "We're in here. We're in the cabinet. Gretchen, the cavalry has arrived."

In a matter of minutes, the metal door flung open. "Gretchen?"

Gretchen blinked twice. *Why does God look like Lily's Devlin Pierce?* "Mr. Delicious?"

He extended a hand out and removed her from her imprisonment. The detective was the next victim to step out into freedom. "Wait, you're Mr. Delicious? I guess I didn't put that together."

Gretchen was busy hugging Dev's neck. He shrugged. Yes. I'm not sure why, but she's always called me that."

"I'll call you anything you want, Agent Pierce." Daniel bent over to stretch his back. "What the heck happened?" The back room looked as though bomb had gone off.

"A lot," Dev answered vaguely. "No guests were robbed. They attempted a heist. I'm thinking a small IED or grenades were used. Gretchen, are you okay? I'm going to have the medics check you two out." He pulled her away slowly and examined her face. "You need some air. Let's get you outside."

As they made their path to the street, Gretchen surveyed the damage to the store. Glass was shattered, and clothing covered the floor. Heels hung from light fixtures and mannequins were strewn in pieces on the escalator. Daniel looked around for his company's team. "Did everyone get out?"

"Yes, detective. No one was seriously hurt. We have Elana in custody, and she's spilling details. In the beginning, she wasn't a willing participant. She has a brother who works with a gang in Miami. I'll fill you in later. The mayor and his wife are fine, and the rare diamonds all left the building before all of it went down." He nodded at Daniel. "The group from the diamond company is just fine."

Daniel was relieved. "What about the bad guys including our little circus performer? I think she smuggled real diamonds out of the building."

"Some reporter was following them, and believe it or not their van broke down."

Daniel would throttle Gretchen later, but her averted eyes led him to believe she knew exactly why the van broke down. "Putnam."

Gretchen clutched at Dev's DEA jacket. He looked around and saw television cameras. "Gretchen, put your face inside my jacket. Neither one of us needs to be on the news at ten."

"Devlin, is Lily here? I need her," Gretchen sobbed.

Dev held her head with one hand while both arms securely held her in his embrace. He led her to the paramedics. "No, she's not, but we're here for you. We'll call her later." Dev managed to hide Gretchen until she was in the security of an ambulance. He tugged on Daniel's jacket. "He needs to be looked at too."

Both victims needed oxygen, but the medics were confident that all the two of them really needed was rest. Gretchen blew her nose. "I'm sure I look like I've been running a marathon in full makeup."

Daniel tucked a loose tendril of her hair behind her ear. "Have you ever run a marathon?"

Her hand waved him off. "Heaven's no! You get too sweaty. I work out in a gym where I can be refreshed by the air conditioning. I don't sweat, I glisten."

Surprised by his own feelings, Daniel needed to kiss her there and then. Spontaneity was her strong suit, not his, but apparently the woman was rubbing off on him. They didn't need a metal cabinet to prove that, but he needed to prove something to her. He grabbed her face tenderly in his hands and looked into her teary eyes. "Gretchen, you glisten all the time. You're the brightest star I know."

Gretchen's head reeled as she saw his lips near hers. Slowly, deliberately, he kissed her. *Maybe I have vertigo? It can't just be him, can it? After all of these years, could he really be the one, a detective in my own city's police force?*

As he pulled back, almost in slow motion, Gretchen noticed his dress shirt was torn. She patted his partially exposed chest. "Daniel, that was very nice, and you did it in front of all of these people."

"Does that matter?" His gray eyes were clear and bright.

"Yes, very much." She wrapped her arms around his neck and returned his affection. "It matters very much to me. Now, when can I go home? I need a very lengthy bubble bath."

"I'll check. I know we'll have to give a statement. I'm not sure if Agent Pierce needs us–"

Gretchen tugged at his pants leg as he stood. "Mister, how long has Agent Pierce been in league with you?"

"It's a long story, but I promise we'll fill you in. Let's do it over a little wine, definitely food, and in the comfort of your own living room."

Gretchen had been deceived by a professional. "So, I'm not the only one who can keep secrets?"

He broke free of her. "But secrets are part of our jobs."

Gretchen huffed in disappointment. "I'm not sure I like a man with secrets."

Daniel crouched down in front of her. "Oh, yes you do, and you will. Trust me."

He left her side before she could continue the verbal sparring she so enjoyed with him. She felt light-headed again, but she also felt giddy. That was an emotion she never enjoyed.

I'm in love for the second time in my life.

Chapter Eighteen

"I'll buzz Agent Pierce in," Daniel volunteered. Gretchen continued chopping an onion and dabbing at her tears. Gretchen sniffed. "I know he likes onions on his steak, but they wreak havoc on my mascara. It's supposed to be waterproof, and it's failing miserably.

The elevator door opened. Daniel's smile faded.

"Detective Williams, this is a surprise." Chance Alexander held a bottle of wine in his left hand and a bouquet of flowers in the other.

"Chance, you're back." He felt like a fool. Gretchen's great love of her life stood in front of him. He could bar him from entry, or he could barricade the apartment door. But where would that get him? "Come on in."

"Hello Mr. Delicious. I have your favorite beer chilling," Gretchen yelled from the kitchen.

"I knew I was special, but I don't think you've ever called me that."

Gretchen's knife was placed slowly on the counter. She removed her glasses and looked up to see a tanned Chance Alexander with gifts in hand. He had her favorite wine and a bouquet of yellow roses. *They mean jealousy!*

"No, I was expecting Lily's husband. He's Mr. Delicious. You've always been, well that doesn't matter. My, this is a surprise." She quickly rounded the counter and came to him. "Are those for me?"

"Who else?" He turned to the detective. "Sorry, Williams. I didn't realize you'd be here."

Daniel felt as though he had faded into the paint. "And I didn't realize you would be either."

Chance handed over his gifts and embraced Gretchen, planting a very quick kiss on her cheek. He wanted the kiss to last longer, but the kiss's recipient pulled away abruptly. "I need to get these into water. Yellow roses aren't the heartiest. Now, my orchids could last for weeks. These are very beautiful. Thank you. And you've brought my favorite wine. That's so sweet that you still remember."

Gretchen's nervous babbling tipped Chance off. He surveyed the kitchen counter. There were three glasses, three plates, and plated appetizers. "I've come at a bad time. I should go."

Daniel and Gretchen exchanged glances, but neither one of them knew what the other was about to say. As Chance exited, Daniel stopped him. "No, you shouldn't."

Gretchen smiled. *Leave it to Daniel to do the right thing.* "You should stay. I want to hear about your beautiful granddaughter, and you'll love our guest. Devlin will be here in a few minutes. We have more than enough food. This is such a pleasant surprise. Daniel, could you please pour Chance a beer? He likes it in a chilled mug."

The use of the pronoun we wasn't lost on Chance. He watched as Gretchen and the detective moved together seamlessly in the kitchen.

In one simple sentence, Daniel had been reduced to an in-home bartender. He was actually thankful when Agent Pierce was buzzed up by an overly helpful Chance. If appearances counted for anything, Chance appeared very much at home, and Daniel felt like a fish out of water.

Gretchen insisted on greeting her guest at the doorway. She outstretched her arms widely. "Devlin, it's so wonderful you could join us."

Devlin Pierce briefly thought about riding the elevator back down and picking up a burger at his favorite place. But his wife would be very disappointed in that behavior. "Gretchen, I brought beer, and Lily told me to bring this pink champagne cake from Phillipe's Sweets and Bakery."

In one rapid movement, the hostess swept him into her arms. "Welcome to the Alpha party," she whispered in his ear.

Dev was helpless, his arms captured by Gretchen's body. He only hoped the cake box would stand up better than he was in the crush. "What is going on?"

Gretchen finally released him and grabbed the box. "Daniel is here, and Chance showed up."

Dev needed a map for this tour of Gretchen's mind. "And Chance is who?"

"The man who got away. My first and only love until—"

Dev's crooked smile was answered by the tapping of Gretchen's heel. "Ah, until the detective, and now they're both here, and you didn't expect that."

"Please come in and save me."

Dev's brow raised. "I never thought I would ever hear you say you needed rescuing from two men."

"I have handled a couple of men in the past, but not these two. I'm blessed with one too many men."

Dev wanted to say so much, but he bit his tongue instead. "I never thought I'd hear you say any of that."

Gretchen pulled on his arm. "Get in here."

After the very awkward introductions, all three men had their beers. Chance and Dev sat at the island while Daniel and Gretchen worked as a team on the meal.

"Daniel, will you get the steaks out? The grill is ready."

Gretchen's upscale kitchen had a built-in gas grill. "I'm actually excited to work on this thing." Gretchen handed him a platter of onions and peppers, while Daniel rubbed spices on the steaks.

Gretchen turned and handed him another plate. "There's zucchini and roma tomatoes, and don't forget to check on the baked potatoes, please."

Dev studied the delicate dance. The detective stepped in one direction; Gretchen turned in another. They moved as a team. Dev wasn't the only one noticing the couple. With a side glance, he noticed Gretchen's first love was now sitting a little straighter. The vein in his neck seemed to be throbbing. Either the man saw what Dev was seeing, or he was in the beginning stages of the mother of all heart attacks. *Lily is going to have a fit when she hears this one. I almost feel sorry for Gretchen. Nah, this is too much fun.*

The best part of the exhibition was that the two didn't even realize how well they worked together, how well they fit and suited each other. And knew each other's needs in advance.

"Chance, what brings you to Kansas City?" Dev asked, hopefully breaking the iceberg that seemed to be doubling in size in the apartment.

"I have a personal security company, and we're handling the protection of

a senatorial candidate."

"Were you ever in the secret service?"

"Yes, but first I was a Marine." His answer elicited a weird noise from Gretchen that seemed to be a mix between a sigh and a snort of disdain.

Dev finished a swallow of beer. "I was always intrigued by the service, but

I ended up in the DEA."

Chance turned to Dev. "Any undercover work?"

"A few years. I've been transitioning into a senior position with a lot more paperwork and fielding questions from politicians."

"That's dangerous work," Chance joked. He turned his attention back to the couple in the kitchen.

Daniel turned as if on cue. He clapped his hands. "Gentlemen, assume your places. We are ready to eat."

Miraculously, the dinner conversation was less tense, but Gretchen found herself being the odd man out as her three guests shared memories of missions and cases.

"So basically, what was going on is that poor Tito and RJ were collateral damage. They both had pieces of the puzzle," Daniel said quietly. "It's such a shame." He stopped briefly. "Well, there were a lot of working pieces. Dev took care of the drug exchange, and our department arrested the security company employees, the entertainers who were involved, and Elana who was the inside connection. She thought the plan was to palm off the real diamonds to the trapeze artist. But she didn't know there were two pouches up in that ice sculpture, the real diamonds Elana placed up there, and the fake ones set in the goblet by Larkin while she was practicing. Gretchen found the hidden key left for the security company. The thieves were only supposed to mess with the security system, but they then had access to the safe. There's really no honor among thieves. Gretchen and I actually spotted them arguing when Elana realized that there was going to be much more to the evening's activities."

Dev nodded. "It all went to hell then. Those diamonds were to be used as payment for the drugs we picked up. This bunch has been doing this in several places around the nation. The drugs came in through Texas, the money and diamonds were funneled through Miami by Elana's brother to several bank accounts in the islands."

"But no one at the event was targeted. We should be thankful for that," Gretchen interjected.

"What were the patterns you two were following?" Chance asked Daniel and the DEA agent.

As the conversation was steered into a party for three, Gretchen excused herself, but no one noticed. She retreated into her bedroom to make a phone call to her "bestie" over a thousand miles away.

"Lily, I need to talk to you."

"Isn't Dev there for dinner?"

"Yes, and two other men."

Lily snickered. "Oh, you must be in heaven."

"You would think so, but the unexpected man is someone I've loved since I was twenty. He just showed up. He's the one handling the security for Marty's campaign."

"Your friend, Marty?"

"You know, the husband of the woman who attempted to frame me for murder. Lily, please."

Lily grabbed a notepad and began to write a list, with Gretchen's name at the top. "I'm ready now. This guy showed up tonight, and you're unhappy about it? I would think you'd throw Dev out and have your way with him."

Gretchen rolled her eyes. "Could you please keep up? This is important."

Lily held the phone away from her face and yelled silently into the night. She calmed herself and continued. "So, what is the problem?"

"There's one more man."

Lily counted on her fingers. "Who?"

"Detective Williams," Gretchen answered flatly.

Lily wrote down the detective's name. Dev told me about him. Oh, the detective who has money, but Gretchen doesn't know!

"He's the man that kisses me senseless." Gretchen sighed.

"And that's a bad thing?" Lily had never heard Gretchen so frantic, so undone. *What magical powers does this detective possess?*

"We have only kissed. I'm becoming extremely frustrated. He hasn't run the bases, if you catch my drift."

Lily giggled. "You always go all in." Lily giggled again at her own joke. "Maybe he's more of a football kind of guy, and you're not in the fourth quarter yet? Oh, wait, I have it. He's a golfer! He takes his time, he shoots eighteen holes on a Saturday, and eventually he'll get that hole in one?" Lily snorted.

"This isn't funny." Gretchen's heels clicked as she moved into the bathroom. She drummed her nails on the counter.

What is that noise? I know I've heard it before. "Gretchen, it sounds like you're very upset. Between the clicking and tapping I can tell. I'm not sure I've ever known someone who had signature sounds like you do."

Gretchen dabbed at a tear. "That is the worst compliment I've ever received. Could we please return to my problem. What am I going to do with these two men?"

Lily stopped smiling. *Gretchen Malloy doesn't know what to do with two men? She's ill, perhaps terminal.* "Gretchen, what can I do for you? Do you need to go to the hospital?"

"No, silly. Lily, what should I do?"

Lily threw her notepad across the room. "Holy Moly. You're in love with the detective! Or you're in love with your former love."

"Yes."

Lily held her head in her hands. "So that is the problem. Let me think."

"You can't for very long. They're going to come looking for me. I'm not sure even Mr. Delicious can save me from this debacle."

"Stop being so melodramatic. Sorry, I forgot I was talking to you. Let's examine this situation. Your former love didn't stay because–"

Gretchen looked into the bathroom mirror. *Why?* "He didn't ask me about the future. He just planned it all out. I had dreams of my own. He married. He had a daughter and now a granddaughter. He left, and now he's back."

Lily fell back on the couch. "Gretchen, will he leave again? Just answer quickly, and don't think about it."

Gretchen drew in a breath and balanced against the cabinet counter. "Yes. That baby is everything to him, and she should be. He'll leave again. He has to, and that's his life."

But my Dev came back to get me. "Okay, now what about this detective?"

"He's old fashioned, and there's something holding him back. I think he has a secret, but Lily, I think I'm in love with him."

"*Mazel Tov,* Gretchen." Lily's Israeli-Arab friend was rubbing off on her. What a story this was! *Gretchen Malloy was in love and not just in lust. God has finally won the war between good and evil, and the world may be coming to an end.* "You love your first love, but you're in love with the detective. Do I have this right?"

"I think so. The more I think about it, I think I'm making myself sick."

Life isn't fair. Gretchen is losing control, and I'm not there to see the miracle. "You are going to go back out there. It's your home so if anyone gets out of line, you just throw them out. You're Gretchen Malloy. You're the best event planner in the city. You're strong and sexy, and you don't need a man. You use them as your play toys."

Gretchen stood taller. She threw her chest out and lifted her chin. "I'm fabulous, seductive, and wiley. I don't need them."

"Yes," Lily cheered. "That's my bestie! Go get them."

"Thanks, bestie. I knew you'd help even though I'm quite certain you've never had two men fighting over you."

And she's back. "Enjoy your night. Tell my husband to call me so I can hear what happened." *And since you just insulted me, I have no inclination to tell you that your detective is worth a mint!*

"Lily?"

"What is it Gretchen?" Lily asked flatly.

"You are a good friend."

"You are too. Hang up before they send a search party."

Gretchen righted herself and strutted into the living room. "Boys, who's up for dessert?"

Dev maintained his composure. Gretchen seductively posed up against the wall leading into the kitchen. Her long red painted fingernails drummed, one of her stilettos tapped impatiently on the wood floor. *I brought the cake for dessert, but I'm not sure that's what she's offering.*

"I'll take a piece," Daniel answered.

"I'm always ready for an after dinner treat," Chance said, adding a wink in her direction.

Devlin Pierce said nothing. He took a drink from his beer. He rubbed his temple. He suddenly had a headache.

Chapter Nineteen

"I said nothing. I ate my piece of cake and had coffee. We all talked, and I went back to my hotel room. I lied and said I had an early meeting today"

"What happened after you left?" Lily asked. She yawned loudly. *Why doesn't this special agent realize how early it was?*

"If I left, I'm not going to know what happened, honey." Dev looked over his calendar as he filled his wife in on last night's festivities. "I'll meet with the detective this morning. Our case is sewn up, but Gretchen and he have to give statements to the KCPD and to the FBI."

"So, if you can't tell me about Gretchen and her men, can you tell me about what happened?"

Dev continued to pull up work emails on his computer while he talked to his wife. "I'll give you the highlights. The detective had his company remove their stock before anything happened. We'd been focusing on the security company, and we discovered that Larkin was a girlfriend of one of those guys. Elana had a family member involved in laundering. We grabbed the drug shipment. Um, Gretchen, the mayor, and her reporter friend did a little of their own investigating which actually helped us in the long run. She even messed with the getaway vehicle, and she had the reporter follow them. Gretchen found the nail that sent us on the trapeze artist's trail; she found the key which sent us on Elana's trail, and she found the medal. She shared her notes with the detective and he realized a pattern of thefts on their diamond courier routes that also blended with huge drug shipments. There you have it."

"Gretchen strikes again. You'll be proud of me. I didn't tell her about how rich her detective is."

Dev shut his laptop and began to pack for the day. "I am proud of you. He hasn't told her yet. I did a deeper dive into him. He's heir to millions, and it's old money. He has his own compound two houses down from an ex-president's place, and he even owns an island in the Caribbean. The best part of this is he's a really nice guy. He's not only generous with his time, but gives to several charities."

"Does he like you? Is he open to adopting a grown woman who would happily watch his beach for him?"

"And Gretchen thinks he's just a detective who works with urban youth and has an old-fashioned sense of chivalry and romance."

"I like chivalry and romance," Lily murmured. "It worked out for me."

"It did, didn't it? Hey, what do you think she's going to do when he tells her?"

Lily cocked her head in thought. "She is a good person. She doesn't care about money or prestige."

Dev grabbed the charging cord for his phone. "I agree. The thing is she isn't really shallow, but she sure gives the pretense of someone who swims in the kiddie end of the pool."

"You've got me there," Lily agreed. "Get your work done and come home. I don't want you anywhere near Gretchen when she realizes you knew the secret."

"Do you think she'll choose one of them? I always had the feeling Gretchen plays it pretty loose, the more the merrier."

"Yes," Lily answered thoughtfully. "But this time her heart is involved in the equation."

Dev looked down at the time. "I've got to get going. I'm sitting in on Gretchen's statement. This should be fun."

"Please film it. I'm begging you."

"It's going to be absolute hell, but I'm not the one leading it. Poor Tom."

By the time Agent Devlin Pierce walked into the FBI offices, Gretchen was sitting comfortably in Tom Fullerton's office. She had her hand over his hand. "It is so good to see you again. I just love FBI men."

"You have to tell the truth, Gretchen. You love all men," Dev commented as he took a chair in the corner of the room.

"Well, that is very true, Agent Pierce."

Tom pulled his hand away and began his interview. "Gretchen, Ms. Malloy, we'll be taking your statement this morning about the event at Laurent's. Let's begin. I'll ask the questions, and you will answer to the best of your ability. Stick to the facts. No extra descriptions are necessary."

Dev silently snickered. He noticed Gretchen had begun to protest, but answered with just a nod. Her young attorney beside her nodded as well.

Two hours later, Dev didn't understand Gretchen any more than he understood how his own wife noticed such useless details. He actually scribbled down a few notes to encourage agents when looking for evidence. One thing was for sure, neither woman ever settled. They continued to dig until they were satisfied with the result of their amateur investigation. *As always, never underestimate Lily or Gretchen.*

"I'll treat everyone for lunch," Gretchen offered as they walked down the hallway of the downtown FBI offices. Her young attorney departed for a court date.

Dev peeked at his watch. He nodded to Tom. "I think we have time. We could meet you somewhere?"

Gretchen beamed with delight. "I know this place, just five minutes away in Briarcliff."

Tom nodded. "I know the one. Dev and I'll see you there."

Gretchen sashayed away, her heels clicking on the marble floor.

Dev frowned as he brushed his hand through his hair. "Why did we agree to lunch with her?"

Tom grinned. "Because we have a death wish?"

After a fairly uneventful lunch where Gretchen talked and the two agents ate, Dev entered his hotel with plans to head to his room to finish an after-action report, and to call his wife. Lily needed to know that Gretchen seemed to be very much in love with the detective, but realized that he had some secret he wasn't sharing. Dev assured her that whatever the detective wasn't divulging probably wasn't a bad thing, and that he would tell her in his own time. But his plans soon changed.

"Agent Pierce."

Dev knew the voice. The detective was standing in the lobby. "Detective Williams, how did your statement go?"

"It was fairly standard," Williams acknowledged. He was dressed for a required day off in jeans, white sneakers, and a pullover sweater. "How did Gretchen do?"

Dev smirked. "Fairly standard when one is Gretchen Malloy. I'm certain yours was less colorful."

The men shared a laugh. "I wanted to speak to you before you bolted home. Can I buy you a drink in the bar?"

Dev read Williams like a book. It was clear he wanted to discuss Gretchen. *Never in a million years did I think I'd be a relationship expert.* "Sure, but let's definitely dispense with the agent and detective stuff."

"I'd appreciate that. I have a table over by the window."

Dev knew the spot very well. It was one of his favorites. When Dev had been assigned to the case involving his future wife, he would sit at this very table and watch the cars and people below at least once a week. A full glass of bourbon was already waiting for Williams.

"Sorry about this. I'm sure you have work to do."

Dev placed his bag on the floor beside him. "I have very little to do tonight and a flight tomorrow that will give me plenty of time. Besides, they serve my favorite bourbon. What can I do for you?"

Daniel waved toward the bar for another bourbon. "I like your directness. I know your wife is very close to Gretchen. I was wondering where I stand with the woman. I know what she seems to want from me, but if that's all she wants then I'm not her man."

Lord, what did I ever do to deserve this? Fine, I'll do it for Lily. If we can keep Gretchen busy with the detective, she won't make any surprise visits to our house. "Daniel, I believe you are exactly who she needs and wants. She's happier than I've ever seen her, and she's less **her**. Does that make sense?"

The bartender placed a glass in front of Dev and the two men toasted. "She's less Gretchen Malloy."

Dev nodded. "She's also less annoying with you in her life. I appreciate that."

Daniel smiled knowingly. "What is that Mr. Delicious thing about?"

"I don't know," Dev answered frankly. "She came up with it, and she'll have to explain it to you." *I'm not about to tell another man that the woman admired my backside.* "But, what do you feel about our Gretchen?"

"At first, I thought she was the most annoying, irritating, fake woman I'd ever met, but on second glance she's extremely caring and generous. She used to give me a headache, and now she gives me a heartache. When Chance showed up the other night, I didn't know what to think. I figured it was over when he left Kansas City a few months ago."

"Daniel, what do you want to give Gretchen?"

He didn't even think about his response. "I want to offer her a life with a little less work. I want her to just enjoy and allow me to pamper her. We talk, we laugh. Her stories are hysterical. I rub her feet. I have no clue why she wears those heels."

Dev laughed. "But you can always hear her coming before you see her, right?" Both men agreed. "My dad once gave me a good talking to after I'd met Lily. He contended that talking and laughing are the most important ingredients in a great relationship recipe. He's right. I've never laughed so much in my life, and I have a companion who shares her opinion and listens to me when I need a sounding board. Do you care about Gretchen?"

Daniel sipped his bourbon. "Very much. I won't hurt her, and I won't walk away unless she thinks that's best."

"Is this a private party, or can anyone join the bourbon club?"

Dev and Daniel looked up to see Chance Alexander pulling up a chair, a bourbon already in his hand. "I would say it's too early to drink, but it is Monday."

"There is that," Daniel answered. "Doesn't the bus trip begin tomorrow?"

"Yes. We'll be on the road until the evening before election day."

"So, you'll be leaving again?" Dev asked casually. He glanced toward Daniel to see if he'd caught his cue.

"Yes, and after the election I head back to Virginia." Chance lowered his head. "So, Williams, what's next in your future?"

Daniel rubbed his glass between his hands. "We were just talking about that. I have a couple of days off, and then it's back to work."

Chance understood. "I've never been one to stay planted or to enjoy the nine-to-five day. You said you were from Boston. Are you planning on making Kansas City your home?"

"I have for a few years now. I love the city and everything about it."

Dev studied the back-and-forth repartee. On first reflection, they were very much the same. Chance was always the guy who was ready for the next assignment or the next mission. The former Marine reminded him of himself just a few short years ago, before Lily. The detective was solid and hardworking. The man was charitable beyond anyone he'd ever met. Dev had deep dived into William's financials and found that he was a good man who used his money to fund various charities and endeavors, including college tuition for ten kids. Both men shared values of integrity and honesty. *Williams needs to tell her his big secret.*

"Gentlemen," Dev announced as he tapped his glass on the table as if he were calling a meeting in session. "We have something, rather someone to discuss. Lily and I, God help us, care about Ms. Gretchen Malloy. Yes, we cringe when she calls with some outlandish story. Yes, we scream in the shower when she surprisingly turns up on our doorstep, but she's our Gretchen. There is no one who can be more loyal or supportive as I'm sure you both know. I believe she cares very much for both of you. Since I believe I'm the only one to be described as Mr. Delicious, I would like to know your intentions. The woman can't go on much longer like this. Spill."

Both men blinked in surprise. One cleared his throat, the other threw back his drink. Chance was the first one to answer.

"I love Gretchen. I always have, and I always will."

Dev glanced to see Daniel's eyes darkening. His despair was obvious. "Daniel, what do you have to say?"

"I." He stopped. "It's personal."

Dev leaned forward. "I know, but I see a woman who cares for two men, and I don't want to see her alone when she has a chance at more happiness. I also don't want to see one man who jumps in and out of her life when he feels like it, and the other ignoring a could-be relationship because of some invented reason."

Dev's low voice was reserved, almost threatening. "Besides, I'll say it again. If she's busy being in love she'll leave Lily and me alone. I'm not sure I ever want to hear that story about the pro football player and the horse again."

Daniel's eyes widened, but Chance chuckled.

"Obviously, Daniel, you haven't heard that one yet," Dev said. "Apparently, Chance has. Well, give it time. You'll be amazed at her flexibility and how she uses the stirrups."

Chance directed his full attention to the younger detective. "The ball is in your court. I told you to always tell her yes."

"Yes." Daniel appeared to look for the answer in the bottom of his glass. "I don't want to see her hurt. She deserves to be cared for, pampered, and even protected when it comes to that. I did that the other night."

Dev's eyes glanced from Chance to Daniel. He saw the answer he wanted and needed to see. He knew the answer, but did they?

Chance flinched and pulled back from the table. "I have a meeting with Marty. Hopefully, he'll be the new senator from Missouri. Detective," he said as he extended his hand, "I'll probably see you now and then." He shook Dev's hand. "Agent Pierce, it was great meeting you. I'm happy that Gretchen has all of you as her family. She's deserved one for a very long time."

He stood and began to walk away. He turned toward Daniel. "Detective, take good care of our girl. Oh, and that age thing…don't worry about it. With age comes wisdom. Besides, a woman over fifty has certain talents that are invaluable."

The silver haired man strutted out of the lobby and seemingly out of the picture. Dev cocked his head. "That went well. You're on your own with the diva of event planners. A few years ago, I might've thought you were crazy for showing any interest in the woman, but now that I've seen her heart on so many occasions, you're a wise man to see her real worth. She can be very pushy. She can be frightening. She insists we have a daughter just for her."

Daniel's wonderment showed on his face. "Yes, she's told me about that. Let's get another round, and you can tell me how that all works."

Dev leaned back in his chair. He looked out onto the street and saw a couple holding hands while strolling on the Plaza. He felt he had just completed negotiations that were more difficult than some he'd had between cartel heads vying over the same shipment of cocaine. Now that he had to explain why he owed a baby girl to Gretchen, he couldn't wait to get back to the real drug lords. It would be much simpler.

Chapter Twenty

"He looks so happy," Gretchen yelled over the cheering campaign workers. Daniel leaned down to hear her.

"It's hard to believe he's the new senator after what he went through with his wife this summer."

Gretchen leaned into her companion and offered a kiss which he happily accepted. "That seems so long ago. Without that fiasco I wouldn't have met you. Love is always worth a little murder."

Daniel shook his head. "Only you can make that sound normal."

Gretchen patted his jacket. "Marty is coming down off the stage. I want to congratulate him."

Gretchen pulled him by the hand through the revelers. Daniel spotted Chance next to the new senator. As they came closer to Marty, Gretchen's grasp on his hand became tighter. Before she came within a handshake of the two men, she let his hand go. Daniel watched as the woman he had been with all night embraced her old friend and her old lover.

"Marty, darling! I told you. You should never doubt me." Gretchen beamed with pride. "You are going to do an amazing job as senator. Chance, will you be going back to Virginia again?"

Chance nodded in Daniel's direction. "Yes, I'll be going back. Marty won't need me full time, and I'll just be a few hours from my girls."

"Yes, your girls." Gretchen turned her attention to the new senator as the two other men were left without a buffer.

"Detective, how is everything?"

"Everything seems fine," Daniel answered. "You're going to be a busy man for the next few weeks."

"Yes, transition time will be hours of work. Marty has a house in mind, and I'll handle the security. My team will be in place by the time he's sworn in. How's it going with Gretchen?"

Daniel's attention was held by the glow of Gretchen's face, and it wasn't just her flashy makeup. Her joy lit up her face. "We're doing well, at least I think we are. I think she's accepted the fact that I like to take it slow."

Chance couldn't contain his shock. "Keep telling yourself, buddy. Gretchen has never been stuck in neutral. If she's taking it slowly, you're in deep trouble."

"Or, she sees this relationship as a lengthy trip, not a short one down to the corner market."

Chance laughed. "You don't know her, but if she allows you to stay around, eventually you'll get there."

Daniel locked his knees and stood at attention. He hadn't done that since the Navy. He was eye-to-eye with a man he saw as a rival. "The difference is, it is her choice, and it will always be her choice in the life she prefers. Ask her to go to Virginia with you. Don't tell her, ask her."

Chance sucked in his breath. His smile faded. "She won't go. I know that now. But if you're daring me, I could."

"You could, but it wasn't in your plans even now, was it?"

Before Chance could answer, Gretchen turned her attention to them. Daniel needed to be rescued, but on second glance it appeared they were involved in a verbal rooster squawk off. "Chance has his life in Virginia, don't you?"

His eyes darted from the detective to the love of his life. One of his loves. "Yes," he answered casually. "You know I'll be back now that I know where you are."

Gretchen cocked her head as though she was staring straight through him. She latched onto Daniel's arm. "You could've always found me, but now that you know where I am, I might not be home. I plan on being very busy. Life certainly takes you in directions you never thought you'd travel."

Daniel raised his finger to interrupt. "We were just talking about travel."

"I love to travel. Where shall we go, Daniel?"

"Right now, I think we should get out of here," he replied calmly. He extended his hand out to Chance despite the grip Gretchen had on his arm. "We will see you soon then?"

Chance softened. "You can count on it, detective."

"I will."

"I will too," Gretchen whispered as she broke from Daniel to place a kiss on Chance's cheek. "Take care of yourself, Marty, and the two loves of your life."

"G, you know I love you," he murmured against her ear.

"I know. I love you too. Have a wonderful life." Gretchen dabbed at her eyes. "You know I'll be having a fantastic life, darling! Tootles!

Chance held her hand tightly. His face was touching hers, and it seemed as though they were the only two in the room. "Gretchen, come to Virginia. Your friend Lily is there. I'm there. We'll have a good life."

Her lips touched his cheeks as she pushed against his chest. "I know where you'll be. And we've already determined where I will be. Please take care of yourself, and who knows? I do love to travel. Goodbye, Chance, at least for now." She pulled out of his hold and picked up Daniel's hand in hers as she walked past her detective.

As they walked away, Gretchen poked her finger into his ribs. "You and Chance were definitely sharing a male moment. I thought you two were going to duel over me. It would be delightful to have two handsome men vying for my hand. I've had dreams about this sort of scenario. Actually, we could play out the fantasy. Did you bring your cuffs with you?"

Daniel's face reddened at her suggestion. "No, I did not. I'm not fighting Chance for you, but we need to talk. Let's go back to your apartment."

Gretchen's heart quickened. *Could this be the night we go back to my apartment to talk, and we just don't go back to my apartment to talk?*

Daniel was adding sugar to his coffee when he invited Gretchen. "I have to go home for a few family discussions, and you could share Thanksgiving with us. You could meet my mother."

Gretchen didn't turn to face him until she could control the look on her face. "Daniel, I spend Thanksgiving here. Although it sounds absolutely wonderful, I have dinner with friends at the club, and then I return home to watch the Plaza lights come on to begin the holidays. Have a wonderful time, and thank you for the invitation." Gretchen grabbed her coffee and headed to the couch. She kicked off her heels into the hallway.

Daniel followed behind. "Wait. I need to tell you something."

"I knew you had a secret. You've had secrets since the day I met you." She placed her coffee down as he sat next to her.

"That was a murder investigation."

"I believe I know your secret."

Daniel's brows furrowed. "Tell me."

"You have some connection to that diamond company. You knew that sweet man who showed me the red diamonds. You could've told me."

Daniel nodded. "You're right. I should've told you, and now I need to tell you something else."

Gretchen's mood changed quickly. She was quite pleased that she knew some part of Daniel Williams' deep, dark secret. "Oh goodie. There's more. Will you offer me your dying love?"

"Yes."

"And then we could…what?"

Daniel felt stripped of all self-respect, but it was worth it to see the look on her face. "Gretchen, heaven help me, but I'm in love with you. I hated how close you were with Chance tonight and how you two shared some whispered endearment. It makes me boil. I love you. But you don't know everything."

Gretchen held her hand up. "Stop. That's enough. You're the sweetest man. If it's any consolation, I always thought you were absolutely fascinating in every way, especially when you walk away. You have the cutest–"

"Gretchen."

"Daniel, we've never even tangoed."

"I do know how to tango."

Gretchen waved him off. "I'm not sure we're speaking about the same thing. I'm not discussing dancing."

Daniel shook his head at another innuendo. "Could you please let me tell you what I need to tell you?"

"Professing your love was enough."

"No, I believe in an honest relationship. I know the pain when one partner lies. I haven't lied. I just haven't told you everything."

Gretchen retrieved her coffee. "I'm listening. I don't know how you can top love, but go for it."

"Gretchen, I knew Ferrity, the nice man who showed you the diamonds because he works for my family's company. We're an old New England family with ties to every lineage society you can name."

"You already explained that to me."

"Gretchen, my business is in finance and the diamond trade. I own the diamond company. I'm the sole heir. My mother's summer house is down the street from an ex-president's compound. We have a two-story apartment overlooking Central Park, and I'll never have to worry about money. Ever."

Gretchen placed her cup on the table. She blinked her eyes as she processed the information. "Ever?"

"Ever."

"Why are you a detective? Wait, did your ex-wife know about the money?"

Daniel lowered his head. "She did. It broke us apart when I wanted to work for a living."

"I see," Gretchen responded slowly. "That could create problems."

"She wanted every designer bag."

Gretchen smiled. "What girl doesn't?"

"She wanted to eat at the best restaurants, be around the best people, and her goal every day was to be seen by this columnist or magazine editor. I understood being seen for her career, but she could never understand my need to give back."

So many thoughts were flowing through Gretchen's mind. She understood both sides of their difficult relationship. "You decided to work as a superhero. You became the sweet detective by day and the avenging philanthropist at night.

Daniel rubbed Gretchen's leg. "I wasn't a detective then. I was in financial investment. My wife and I followed different paths, and when she cheated on me, I shut down. I didn't care about having anyone to share a meal with or to talk to at the end of a long day. But then I met you."

"Love at first sight?" Gretchen asked hopefully.

"I can't say I fell in love with you instantly. As you recall, I wanted to put you in jail."

"Yes, for just about anything, but I wore you down, Daniel." Daniel nodded. "You're worried that your money will get in the way of you ever having a healthy relationship? Is that it?"

Daniel looked directly into her eyes. "I suppose so."

Gretchen's giggle unnerved him. "I can honestly say that I won't allow your money to bother me! I can spend with the best of them, but I spend my money. There's no better feeling except for a very strong friendship or even a man who promises undying love."

Daniel placed his finger on her lips. "I didn't say undying. You said that."

"But, you agreed to it. Done and done."

Gretchen's eyes fixed on his. *I'm used to men pretending they have money and discovering they don't, and that's never stopped me from having a wonderful time.*

Daniel stood up suddenly. "Wait, you said something about friendship? Aren't we more than that?"

"Daniel, don't be so serious. What would you call the relationship we have? We kiss. I literally shake from your absence, but you've been holding back because you judged me. You thought I'd be like your wife. We haven't even waltzed."

"If waltzing is another word for what I think it is, let me be clear. I love you. I don't understand it. We are different people. I don't want to change you. I don't want to just be lovers. I want to be loved and to love. I think it's time for me to say goodnight."

Before Gretchen could respond, Daniel Williams bolted from the couch, grabbed his winter coat, and had his hand on the doorknob.

"Wait, just wait." Gretchen lost her balance as she rounded around a chair and fell into his arms. "Daniel, you saved me."

"I wasn't going to just let you face plant," he growled. "I'll call you tomorrow when my head is clearer."

"Stop. You saved me."

Daniel couldn't take anymore tonight. "I know. You lost your balance. You're welcome."

Gretchen stomped her bare foot. There was clicking, but the thud on the floor made Daniel throw his attention back to her face. "Detective, you seem to always save me. No one has ever done that for me. I haven't allowed many to really get past the lashes, the lips, the hair, and even the shoes in a very long time. Lily, Abby, Devlin, and a handful of others see me, but you tore me down. You are the one who makes me safe. I want–”

Daniel clutched her shoulders. “Gretchen, it’s okay. We can talk tomorrow.”

Her gaze fell on those gray eyes and full lips. “I can’t tell what the future might be for us. With my age you know we won’t need to move near a school, and with your dangerous job, I could outlive you.”

Her humor always broke down a dire situation. Williams smiled. “I will probably die before you. You’ll wear me out.”

Gretchen narrowed her eyes and licked her lips suggestively. “If you’re lucky, mister. I fear that you are the one. I think I’ve been denying that from the day I met you. Daniel, I can’t believe it either, but I think I’m in love with you too.”

“Are you sure? It’s okay if you don’t feel like I do.”

Gretchen patted his face gently. “My sweet man. It’s better if I do feel the same way, for both of us.”

They talked for hours until Daniel finally left that night. Gretchen slowly turned down the sheets on her very large, empty bed, and prepared for another very long cold shower.

Chapter Twenty-One

"Did you pack for seven days?"

"Yes, Daniel. The last thing you said when you left last night, on New Year's Eve I might add, was to pack for seven days and seven nights. You have also mentioned copious amounts of times that warm weather will be involved. I even packed this red sarong with a butterfly pin–"

"Gretchen, the car is waiting for you downstairs. Stop talking and get to the airport."

Gretchen stuck her tongue out at her cell phone. "Daniel, we had such a lovely night, don't ruin the first day of the bloody year!"

"I'm sorry. I know you're tired, but you can sleep on the plane."

"Fine. I'll tell you all about my fabulous wardrobe when you're held captive on the flight."

"And you have your passport?"

"Yes, Daniel. Please stop talking so I can hang up on you properly. Either way, I'm hanging up. This early flight on New Year's Day is a first for me so it better be worth it."

"I can't hear you. I'm hanging up now. Goodbye, darling."

Gretchen frowned at the phone. "He just hung up on me. That man." If someone had told her she would be beginning this year jetting away to some warm destination with a wonderful man like Daniel, she would've thought they had too much champagne. As she headed out of the lobby, the driver hurried to grab her bags. Snow was beginning to fall. Gretchen pulled her wrap closer as she entered the vehicle. She loved a good limousine. This one seemed to have every accessory a girl could want, but she decided to get a few more things done. She texted a client about her upcoming Valentine's Day wedding as the car traveled through the downtown area. *Why didn't the driver take the highway to KCI?* She put her phone and glasses away.

"Excuse me. Why are you taking this ramp? This goes to the Wheeler airport," Gretchen commented.

"It's okay, Ms. Malloy."

"No it isn't. We're flying out of the country. We need to be at Kansas City International."

Despite her tone of authority, the driver completely disregarded her advice. She texted Daniel, and he only answered that everything would be fine. The driver parked the car near an entrance to the airport. Another gentleman waited to retrieve her bags. "Ms. Malloy, I'll take you to Mr. Williams."

Gretchen walked slowly. Even though it was cold, her uncertainty made her doubt this entire trip.

"We're right here."

Gretchen looked to see a small set of steps attached to a private jet. There was a short red carpet and a young lady with a large smile who was shivering as she waited for her only passenger. "Welcome Ms. Malloy, and happy New Year! We'll load your luggage and then prepare for takeoff before this weather strands us here. I'm Jessie, by the way."

Gretchen put on her professional face. "Jessie, thank you. Is Detective Williams pranking me, and we're just going to a hotel with a hot tub?"

"Oh, no. He's just completing his final check. Let's get you out of this weather. I have coffee ready. I'll serve breakfast once we're up in the air."

As soon as Gretchen entered the warmth of the cabin, she began to examine the interior. She saw an interior filled with over ten luxurious leather chairs, small tables in between the seating, and two sofas at the back of the plane.

"You may sit anywhere. I have your coffee."

Gretchen was surprised by Jessie's attentiveness. *Aren't there other passengers?* She removed her wrap and chose the seats in what would be the second or third row in a commercial plane. "I'll be fine here." Jessie placed the coffee cup on the table in front of her.

"Ms. Malloy, we have films and live television as soon as we're up, or it's always a good time for a nap. I've never been fond of early flights."

Gretchen wiggled in the massive seat. She took a drink of coffee. "This is good. The nap sounds like a fine idea, and I've never been fond of this time in the morning either. I was just at a party only a few hours ago." *And conversing with that mysterious Daniel! Where is that man?*

The door of the cockpit was slightly ajar. She saw one pilot. The attendant returned to explain the flotation devices, the oxygen, and the seat belt which clipped differently than Gretchen was used to when traveling. "Ms. Malloy, I'd be happy to make you a mimosa or maybe a bloody Mary?"

"Either sounds magnificent, but Jessie, my name is Gretchen. I'm on vacation. At least I was told I was on vacation, so I'm just Gretchen."

"You are on the best kind of holiday, Gretchen. I have a few safety checks of my own, but I'll return as soon as we're up. Have a great flight."

"Hopefully, we'll all have a great flight," Gretchen added. Jessie left to go to the rear of the plane as the door upfront opened wide to reveal a smiling Daniel Williams. He directed someone outside, and the exterior door was closed. He turned to see the face of the woman he loved. She was dressed as if she was headed to Paris for fashion week. Her red sweater dress accented her curves just right; her tall stiletto heel boots passed her knees.

With hands outstretched, Daniel yelled, "Surprise."

"I detest surprises unless I'm planning them. Where are we going? How did you steal this corporate jet, and where is everyone else? I'm not feeling comfortable about this entire trip to only God knows where."

"Wow, you are a hard sell." Daniel sat across from her. "Everything is above board."

Gretchen's tone suddenly lightened. "You won the silent auction for the trip to the Bahamas, didn't you? Do we change planes in Atlanta? I'd like to get some gum."

"We'll make a stop in Atlanta to refuel, and I'll have someone get you gum. In fact, Jessie may have some on the plane."

Gretchen leaned over to whisper. "You did win the trip, right?" When Daniel shook his head negatively, she stomped her feet even though she was seated. "Daniel, I want answers."

"Fine. You won't be happy until you know everything. Here's your answers. We are going to a very special private island in the Bahamas that is owned by me. Jessie and Chad, the other pilot, are employees of my company. They work for my family's corporation, and this is one of our private jets. You are stuck with me for the next week, except for the family who lives on the island. They're supposed to be our staff, but they're more like family to me. We can do anything or nothing at all for seven days. Now, I have to get us up off the ground." He stood and kissed her cheek. Before he could escape, she reached out for him.

"You don't just have money, you have **money.** Fine, I'll play along this one time, but I'll not indulge your fantasies ever again."

Daniel kissed her hands. "Gretchen, I was counting on you to indulge all of my fantasies this week."

"Daniel, you're attempting to act like me. You sound like you're seducing me. You don't need to do that. I've known that I wanted you since the first time you kissed me."

He kissed her hands one more time before turning to the cockpit. "Good. It seems like we're both finally on the same page. We'll have time, plenty of it." He stopped and walked back to her. He whispered in her ear. "I've arranged for us to use the master bedroom, if that's okay with you."

Gretchen nodded quickly. "Is there just one bedroom, Daniel?"

"No. If you get tired of me, there's five others and two cabanas by the pool. I'm flying this part of the trip so enjoy the flight and rest. I'll see you in Atlanta." He kissed her cheek and entered the cockpit.

"I better get more than a bag of peanuts, mister."

Daniel pretended not to hear her protestations. As he sat down to prepare for takeoff, he was still chuckling. "I have my hands full with her."

"If anyone can handle her, you can Danny boy," Chad the co-pilot chided. "Does she know what she's getting into with you?"

"She doesn't have a clue."

"Chad, could you close the door? She's telling that football player story again. If Jessie is lucky, Gretchen will get a case of laryngitis before she gets to the one about the snowstorm in Denver." Daniel shook his head and concentrated on the gauges and buttons in front of him.

Jessie sat across from Gretchen. "And then I took the football and–"

Jessie laughed uncontrollably at the story of the rendezvous with the professional football player in the middle of a massive snowstorm in Denver. "You mean you spent days at the airport with him?"

Gretchen winked. "And I mean **with** him."

It was already an hour into the flight, and Gretchen had enjoyed a lovely breakfast of eggs, bacon, and an English muffin accompanied by a rather large mimosa. Jessie and she were becoming fast friends.

Daniel entered the cabin, a small cup of coffee in his hand. "Are you telling her about the soccer player encounter?"

"It's the story about the blizzard layover in Denver."

Daniel ignored her sexual inuendo. "He was a wide receiver, right?"

Gretchen winked at Jessie. "He definitely was a receiver."

Daniel shook his head. Why didn't it bother him that she spoke so freely and with such zeal about her past? He knew why. She was with him now. "We have less than an hour to Atlanta so I'll see you after we land."

"That's fine. Jessie and I are having a great time. Women always have something to talk about."

"And if they're Gretchen Malloy, they talk and talk," he murmured as he headed back to his domain.

"And they can hear too, Daniel!"

Jessie giggled at her boss and his friend. "Is there anything else I can get you? Mr. Williams mentioned you needed gum. I have some in the galley."

"Wonderful. How do I get into the WIFI? I'd need to research something."

"Just turn on your device, and you'll see the prompts. I better see if they need anything up there."

With Jessie gone, Gretchen retrieved her tablet from her bag and began her search. *Why didn't I do this before? The first time I don't do a background check on someone, and he ends up being a fraud.* There were pages of internet information on the diamond company. There were pages on the Williams family, and then there was Daniel's photo as CEO and Chairman of the Board. Another man was currently the acting CEO. There was even a mention that Daniel Revere Williams supported law enforcement and was a philanthropist. He was an Ivy League graduate with a master's degree in International Economic and Social Finance. His hobby was boxing. He was divorced. Jessie came through the cabin, and Gretchen shut her device down. *What would I have done differently if I'd known all of this?*

Gretchen took a few minutes to mull it all over in her brain. She'd been with powerful people. She'd enjoyed the company of handsome men and beautiful women. But as she looked around the cabin, she was taken back. No wonder she'd been off balance all these months. *Perhaps Daniel has more stories than me?*

Gretchen closed her eyes to think, but instead of figuring out what the man was all about, she fell asleep. The next time she opened her eyes, Jessie was sitting across from her.

"How long did I sleep?"

"Just look out the window and see."

Gretchen's eyes squinted at the brightness of the sun casting its glow on the different shades of azure, aquas, and greens of the Caribbean. Small islands dotted the water.

They were beginning a descent. Gretchen quickly slid over into the window seat and rebuckled.

The plane circled a cove with its own white sand beach. There seemed to be an estuary on the other side of the island with birds' nests clearly visible from the air. As they made their approach to land, Gretchen saw a pool with two hot tubs, tennis courts, the cabanas, and surprisingly, a stable with horses grazing in a small fenced area. The main house was stark white with palm trees and colorful landscaping encircling it. There were orchids everywhere.

"Oh my."

"It's paradise, isn't it?" Jessie asked. "He just had all those orchids planted for some reason. They are stunning."

Gretchen knew the reason.

As Daniel landed the plane, he heard clapping from the cabin. Gretchen's sunglasses were perched on her face, and she was standing when he came to her side. "Are you ready?"

"Yes, and those orchids were a nice touch. I can't wait to see that house. Do you have a designer? I can do so much with so little. Seriously, I once had to decorate an entire wedding reception with flowers I picked up at a nearby cemetery."

"You are kidding, right?" he asked as he led her down the steps.

"Sadly, no. You know I never exaggerate or lie."

"I'm beginning to believe that is the most frightening trait you have, Gretchen."

Chapter Twenty-Two

"I can safely say that this day has made me forget any bad memories surrounding this holiday," Daniel admitted. They had just completed eating a lovely lobster dinner on the patio and were sitting on the dock with a bottle of champagne. Gretchen's bare feet swung free of any stiletto heels.

The woman beside him placed her arm over his shoulder and snuggled into his body. "I have to admit, I don't care about money, but it is nice to be pampered like this. Fabulous becomes me, doesn't it?"

"It does indeed. You look like you belong here."

Gretchen played with his hair that hung over the collar of his shirt. "I belong where you are. I have never felt so safe and satisfied in my life. I think it was the coconut pie for dessert. Oh, and the vases filled with orchids throughout the house certainly made me very happy."

Daniel patted her leg. "Really? All I had to do was feed you pie and lobster, and give your orchids? Even though we haven't–"

"Yes, even though! But I have great hopes for that. I'm satisfied, content with who I am, and who I am with."

"No more outrageous Gretchen? No more clicking on windows or clacking of heels? No more drumming of nails or crazy stories about this man or that event?"

Gretchen's throaty laughter filled the quiet of the night. "Oh, Daniel, don't be silly. I will continue to click, clack, drum, talk, and walk in high heels until I break my neck, I fear."

"Look." Daniel pointed to a shooting star flying across the sky. As their faces were mere inches from each other, he took the opportunity to capture her face to kiss her. She caught her breath and said nothing when he released her.

"Are you still breathing? Can you still talk?"

Gretchen's eyes remained closed as she relished the taste of him. He literally took her breath away creating a time when there really wasn't anything to be said. Except. "Holy Moly."

Daniel's smile faded as she kissed her again, eliciting a similar response. "Gretchen, I have plans to leave you breathless and speechless the rest of your life. That way I won't have to hear those ridiculous stories."

She nodded like an obedient schoolgirl.

"I also plan on spoiling you because you really can just be happy with the simplest of things." Daniel reached over to his jacket on the dock. He retrieved a small light blue box. "But nothing simple tonight. Don't get too excited with the box. I only bought the chain there."

Gretchen knew the jeweler's box very well. Every girl dreamed of a light blue box of their own. "Daniel!

We've discussed that we wouldn't give each other gifts." He placed it in her hand, and she opened it slowly. Gretchen clutched at her throat.

"Do you like it? It's the red diamond you selected the night of the event."

"I'll need guards around me when I wear it. It's lovely, but you can't afford this." Gretchen slid her finger over it. It seemed unreal.

"I can, in fact Ferrity was thrilled that I finally wanted something from the company. It has been years. Now, that diamond isn't perfect, but–"

Gretchen kissed him fiercely. "It is perfect, besides it's in my color and who could possibly wear it as well as I will? But why?"

"I'm attempting to buy your love just in case I don't meet your standards tonight." Daniel nodded back to the bedroom at one end of the house.

I doubt you could disappoint me even if you were in a coma. "You do know I'm a very experienced woman."

Daniel nudged her arm. "That's what I've heard over and over."

Gretchen closed the box, stood up, and gathered her shoes. It is way past time. "Daniel, let's go make some memories."

Daniel looked up at her with large eyes. "Promise me I won't become one of your stories."

"I'm not sure I can promise that. You see, I'm Gretchen Malloy, and I have a certain status to maintain."

"I'll always be the lowly, old-fashioned detective." He grabbed his jacket as he walked next to her.

"No, you'll be the man I love."

He moved his arm possessively across her back. "The diamond won you over, didn't it?"

"Of course, well and the plane, the staff, the island, the orchids, the pool, the beach, the boat, and the horses. I don't think I've gone for a ride on the beach in years, well I mean with a horse not–"

Daniel's head began to hurt, but luckily for him a sudden downpour began that shut down Gretchen's lingering memories of a man named Nico on the island of Mykonos. By the time they reached the living area of the house, they were drenched.

Removing the diamond necklace from the box, Gretchen turned to Daniel. "Will you put it on me?"

"Of course." He took the delicate jewelry from her and latched it at the back of her neck. He sealed it with a kiss. "I'll need to get your earrings next."

Gretchen turned so he could admire it. "Daniel, you are soaked." She slowly unbuttoned his wet shirt and pulled it from his waistband, leaving his chest bare to her roving eyes. *My detective, I won't just talk about us, I'll boast.* "We need to get out of these wet clothes."

Naturally, she led him into the bedroom. Daniel began to fiddle with a lamp, but she pulled him away. "No light tonight."
"What are you afraid of?"

"I don't want to disappoint you. Give an older woman her pride."

Still holding hands, Daniel kissed her. "That doesn't matter. Nothing can stand between us now."

Gretchen pushed up against him. "Mister, the only thing between us tonight will be this little necklace. Mr. Old-Fashioned, where do we begin?"

Daniel threw his shirt onto the floor. He lowered his head and brushed her lips with his. He moved onto her right ear. "You definitely need earrings." His attention was caught by the hollow of her throat, just above where the necklace set. "I need to remove this very long shirt thingy."

Gretchen rolled her eyes. "It's a tunic, Daniel. It's just hanging on my shoulders. One tug should–"

The detective was a quick study. The loose fabric was pooled at her feet. "Do we have whipped cream in the refrigerator?"

Daniel's trail of kisses had traveled well below the red diamond. "You won't need it," he murmured.

"Do you have any of that pie left?"

Daniel's head lifted quickly. "Oh come on. You're not really going to use the pie in the bed, are you?"

She lightly tapped his bare shoulder. "No, silly. Get your mind out of the gutter. I'm actually hungry."

Daniel pretended to stagger in shock. "After all of these months, you want to eat dessert first?"

Gretchen admired his body as the moonlight highlighted it in the darkness. "Daniel, I don't know why I'm stalling."

Daniel returned to take her into his arms. "It's frightening being in love, but trust that we are good together. I won't leave unless you tell me that's what you want."

"So you admit we're a good team?"

Despite his better judgment, Daniel agreed. "You are my partner."

She lightly traced his lips with her finger. "Um, the whipped cream would be interesting. You should see how it enhances–"

"Stop. Could we just enjoy each other without props tonight?"

"I suppose. But don't become an old curmudgeon. Live a little."

"Tell me in the morning," he murmured against her cheek. He began to walk her toward the bed. "We have all night to begin this new year."

The next morning, Daniel Williams felt completely at peace as he dried off on the beach after his swim. He hadn't felt this free in over a decade. He waved at Jonah, the head of the family on the island.

"Daniel, the fishing was good. Do you and your lady friend want a few for dinner?" He held a net full of lobsters. "I speared these beauties."

"I don't want to take away from your family."

"I have plenty, besides the wife wouldn't forgive me if I didn't share with you. When she gave your lady the tour, she noticed you haven't seemed this happy since before the war."

Daniel figured he was discussing actual combat, but the last time he'd brought his ex-wife to the island, a war of words had erupted that began a downward slide. "A lobster salad would be good for lunch."

"I spotted grouper off the north side of the island. If you don't need the boat today, the boy and I will go out. You could treat your lady to a Bahamian treat, maybe add rice and beans. I made sure you have the spice in the cupboard."

Daniel took the net. "You take the boat. My plans are to just stay by the pool."

Jonah smiled. "Good for you. It's just another day in paradise."

As Daniel closed in on the house, he could see Gretchen moving around in the kitchen. Her hair was pulled back in a ponytail, her reading glasses perched on her nose. When he opened the glass doors, he noticed the sneakers on her feet. "What are those?" He pointed down.

Gretchen smirked. "They're sneakers. I forgot my slippers. I woke up alone in that big bed so I'm not in the best mood. What are those?" She pointed at his catch.

"Lunch. Sorry about the empty bed, but it seems you survived."

"Darling, I'm like a cockroach. I'll always survive. They are moving."

Daniel smiled like a child showing his teacher the frog he caught. "Yep. I'll move them into the sink in the butler's pantry."

Gretchen filled two cups with coffee. *I can always figure out a coffee maker, even one that has all the bells and whistles.* She grabbed the eggs from the refrigerator as Daniel returned to the kitchen. He leaned over and placed a kiss on her cheek then leapt up on the counter.

"Are you actually cooking?"

It is the first time in forever. "I cook. What do you want in your omelet? I have veggies, ham, and cheese."

"That's perfect." He watched her work. Gretchen was unusually quiet. He studied her as though she was a murder suspect again. Was she angry or disappointed? Was last night what she wanted, or was he not who she needed?

"Will you take the plates and silverware, please?" She asked as she placed the omelets onto the plates that already held sliced fruit and toasted muffins.

"Yes, ma'am," Daniel answered. He didn't look back as he headed toward the table poolside. He called her by the name that shouldn't be said. She was probably grabbing a knife and deciding if she would dig it into his back or wait and surprise him with a full-frontal attack.

Still, she said nothing. "Daniel, could you please bring the coffee and juice?"

The attentive server seemed to please her as he sat down across from her. "What would you like to do today?"

"I haven't had much time to think. Obviously, you've already gone for a swim and have decided what we're having for lunch."

Daniel felt a cold rush up his back. There it was. She hadn't been advised, nor given her consent. "I'm sorry. I always swim every morning when I'm down here, and

Jonah had just caught those beauties. The week is yours to decide. This is all for you."

Gretchen raised a quizzical brow. She took a moment to examine the situation. She had made breakfast for this man. She'd slept in his arms all night, and she hadn't bothered to wake up early to attach her eyelashes or put on one spot of makeup. *This is nice.* "All for me? This place, the food, the gifts, and even you?"

This Gretchen Malloy was so much easier to read. *I can see her eyes clearly without the tarantula eyelashes?* She was toying with him. "Yes, all for you. I hope I wasn't too old-fashioned last night."

"Oh, you'll do, and I can train you."

Daniel continued to enjoy his breakfast. "Do tell, ma'am."

So you want to play? You are with the queen of amusement. "Daniel, this week I'd like to frolic. That's an old word for someone old-fashioned. I'd like to ride a horse on the beach, swim, fish–"

Daniel chuckled.

"Seriously, I love to fish. I go to the lake quite a bit in the summer. Of course because of you, I missed my fishing this past year. We can use the boat–"

"Not today. I told Jonah his son and he could have it. They're going after grouper."

Gretchen's fork struck the edge of her plate. "I'd love to go. Do you think you could ask them?"

"You really want to go?"

"Yes, a nice boat ride would be just the thing, besides, I'm a little tired this morning."

"Really? I thought you slept pretty well. My arm fell asleep, but you were snoring away."

Her tone changed immediately to its own imitation of an imperial queen, one who could cut off your head. "I do not snore."

"Yes, you do."

"No one has ever complained before," she spat out.

Daniel stood up quickly. "If I didn't think that the robe you're wearing is silk, I'd throw you in that pool. No one has ever complained because they don't stay longer than for a cup of coffee in the morning," he muttered as he picked up several dishes and walked away.

"And you're very predictable," she called out after him. She smiled. There wasn't one thing wrong with him, not one muscle. *Who am I kidding? He'll have to shove me out with a long pole covered with fire ants to move me from his side.*

Gretchen heard the dishwasher. Water was running in the kitchen sink. *He can't be avoiding me, can he? That's not Daniel's style.* She couldn't take it any longer as she walked back into the house. Daniel's head was stuck in the refrigerator.

"What are you doing?"

"I'm checking out our supplies. I'll make you a drink later that will knock your socks off. We'll name it **The Gretchen**. But first, I'll show you old-fashioned.

As Daniel continued his search, Gretchen tapped her glasses on the counter. She began to tap with her fingernails. Still, no response. "Daniel!"

"Since you have a particular appetite, I was thinking about experimenting," he finally answered. "Here it is." His smile was wide as he presented the tub of whipped cream. "I'm thinking this will make you happy."

"We don't need that," she answered flatly. "You don't need that. *It's never felt so good sleeping in someone's arms.*

He acted shocked to his core. "Last night was to your majesty's liking? I was okay?"

Gretchen scrunched her nose in protest. "Now you're just fishing for compliments."

Daniel opened the lid of the container and dipped his finger in. He tasted it. "I don't know, this is pretty sweet. Maybe we should try honey?"

"I didn't realize you have an appetite for sweets, and that you can be so very obnoxious. You know darn well that last night was amazing. Is that what you want me to say?"

Daniel leaned against the counter, reaching across to gather her hand in his. "I don't need that, but I was wondering about the way you were acting."

"What can I say? I'm not a morning person when I've been kept up all night."

"We can go out with Jonah, have a little lunch, and nap by the pool."

"That sounds like the perfect day. Daniel, I fear you are going to take up quite a bit of my time. I hadn't realized you were so needy."

His gray eyes bore into her soul. "And you thought you were the high maintenance one?"

Gretchen pulled her hand away and feigned indifference. "That's ludicrous. Oh, by the way, I've been thinking about our age difference. I've decided I won't let your immaturity bother me." She smiled after her coy statement.

Daniel accepted her challenge and began to search the cabinets.

"Now what, Daniel?"

"I'm looking for honey."

You are going to be a handful, aren't you dear man? She came to his side and closed the cabinet. She took his hand. "We don't need honey. Call your man, and tell him we're going fishing. Let's get dressed."

As they headed for the bedroom, Daniel texted Jonah. "We'll meet them at the dock by ten."

Gretchen pulled him close for a kiss. "That's perfect timing."

"Let me get the honey," he kidded.

She looped her arms around him. "No, we only need the two of us. Besides, everyone knows honey is just too sticky."

"Then we can take a long shower," he suggested. She shook her head. "You know, with you in those sneakers you're nice to have in my arms this way."

"I would never have thought that."

Daniel was confused. "Well, when you add five or six inches with those blasted heels–"

"Oh, not that. I never thought anyone would say I was nice. Naughty perhaps, but never nice."

Daniel laughed out loud as Gretchen pulled away to begin to dress. "Gretchen, let's keep that little secret to ourselves, shall we?"

Gretchen began to return with a witty retort, but she heard yelling.

"Mr. Daniel. My boy is missing."

"Jonah. I should go out there." Daniel quickly exited through the bedroom sliding doors with Gretchen two steps behind.

"Jonah, what's happened?"

The frantic father held a note in his hand. "My boy is gone. He's been kidnapped."

Daniel grabbed the note and began to read. He passed it onto Gretchen.

"Do you have a clue what is going on, Jonah?"

"No, Daniel. Maybe he got himself into trouble? It's a mystery to me. Will you help me?"

Daniel's eyes met Gretchen's.

"Of course we'll help," Gretchen answered. "We're very good at solving mysteries together."

"But we were supposed to do what you wanted to do," Daniel reminded.

"But I want to do this. Please, Daniel? We must help him."

He gazed over at his friend who needed their assistance desperately. "Gretchen, I'll always tell you yes. Jonah, when was the last time you saw him? Has he been on one of the larger islands in the past couple of days? Has he been acting differently?"

Luckily, Gretchen had her readers in her pocket. She read over the note and noted the words "Popi" and "Man" had been used. *This isn't written by a mastermind.* On closer review, the writing looked as though a nervous teenager had written it quickly, either under duress or to gain attention. But she wouldn't state the obvious just yet. She admired Daniel. As he asked his questions, Gretchen knew she was where she should be, and who she should be with…with her detective on another mystery.

Notes From the Author

Leave it to Gretchen Malloy to discover love and mystery on on exotic island. (Usually, I only acquire a tropical drink or two and a sunburn.) Gretchen is also partnered with an unexpected man, someone who surprises her almost on a daily basis. While our favorite planner uses shopping as therapy (many of us do), her detective bids on items at a charity event even though he can fly her off in his own private plane.

There's just something about the Stiletto Terrorist that draws me in. I'm not sure I've ever met a woman who would describe herself as fabulous, seductive, and wiley. That's a perfect package of femininity. Gretchen's confidence can be overpowering, but it can also be admirable. What a woman! I could use a touch of that bravado. However, it's reassuring that even a woman like Gretchen can have a doubt or two in her life. What about you? Are you fabulous? Have you gone along for a while only to head in a completely different direction? I'm still not wearing those heels!

Obviously, the new lovers are already on another adventure. We'll see where it takes them. Of course, Gretchen will always come to Lily's rescue and renew their partnership occasionally in *The Lily List Mystery Series.*

So for now...**Tootles!**

C.L. BAUER

C.L. Bauer lives in Kansas City, Missouri. Her first novel *The Poppy Drop, A Lily List Mystery* was well received by the top 100 Books of Independent Publishers when it launched in 2018.

The series features the highly organized, post-it note, and list making florist Lily Schmidt. Readers have enjoyed the mysteries and the characters who come in and out of her life. Ms. Bauer draws on true events from her family's wedding and event flower business. With over one hundred years of serving families on their special days, Clara's Flowers has received numerous awards in the wedding world, including "best of" and "legacy winner" for service and design.

With a background in journalism and communication, C.L. Bauer has returned to her first love of writing. Currently, *The Lily List Mysteries and The Exclusive Series* keep her busy. Her upcoming projects include more cozy(ish) adventures with Lily and friends, a memoir of her father's World War II days, a psychological thriller, and a mystery/thriller series based on the history of her hometown.

C.L. Bauer loves to interact with her readers. She'll accept invitations from book clubs for in-person appearances or virtual ones. You can contact her through her pages on Facebook, Instagram, Twitter, Pinterest, Netgalley, and Goodreads.

Join her monthly newsletter by signing up on her website www.clbauer.com or email her at clbauerkc@gmail.com. As always…Happy reading!

www.ingramcontent.com/pod-product-compliance
Lightning Source LLC
Chambersburg PA
CBHW070511160726
48003CB00004B/1526